Alon mask - Hero, Flawed Genius, or Something In Between?

Anshumala Singh

Published by Anshumala Singh, 2024.

This is a work of fiction. Similarities to real people, places, or events are entirely coincidental.

ALON MASK - HERO, FLAWED GENIUS, OR SOMETHING IN BETWEEN?

First edition. September 23, 2024.

Copyright © 2024 Anshumala Singh.

ISBN: 979-8224616138

Written by Anshumala Singh.

Alon Mask: The Mask Man of the Modern Era

Disclaimer

Dear Readers,

Thank you for picking up *Alon Mask: The Mask Man of the Modern Era*. This book is a fictional take on a character whose life mirrors some of the most influential, visionary, and yes, controversial figures of our time. Through the character of Alon Mask, I wanted to explore the complexities of innovation, power, and ambition in the modern world.

In today's fast-paced society, leaders and creators often walk a thin line between hero and villain, and Alon is no exception. His journey will take you through moments of incredible success, sharp criticism, and ethical dilemmas. But more than anything, this book is about understanding the man behind the mask—the person whose ideas have shaped the world we live in, for better or worse.

I hope this story offers you a fresh perspective on the balance between progress and responsibility, as well as a glimpse into the pressures that come with being a visionary in the public eye.

Enjoy the journey, and let's see where Alon Mask's path takes us.

Warm regards,

Anshumala Singh

Author of *Alon Mask: The Mask Man of the Modern Era*

Preface

The world we live in today is one driven by technology, innovation, and the relentless pursuit of progress. At the forefront of this movement are individuals who dare to dream big and push boundaries. But with great ambition comes great controversy. This book is a fictional exploration of one such individual, Alon Mask, whose life reflects the triumphs and challenges faced by modern-day innovators.

Alon Mask is not just a character; he is a symbol of the modern entrepreneur—the dreamer who revolutionizes industries, disrupts norms, and divides opinions. In creating this character, I have drawn inspiration from real-world events and personalities, but the story is purely fictional, designed to spark thought and conversation about the impact of those who lead with bold ideas.

Throughout this book, you will encounter different facets of Alon Mask's life—from his groundbreaking ideas to the controversies that follow him wherever he goes. Each chapter delves into a significant event or decision in Alon's career, presenting not just his success but also the fallout and questions that arise. The companies, technologies, and controversies you'll read about—such as Jitter, MaskX, and Bitmask—are fictionalized versions of real-world concepts, adapted to highlight the complexities of being a global influencer in the digital age.

This story is not about judging right or wrong. It's about understanding the nuances of leadership, innovation, and the responsibilities that come with power. Alon Mask, in all his brilliance and flaws, represents the struggle between pushing humanity forward and dealing with the consequences of that push.

I invite you to take this journey with an open mind, reflect on the lessons it offers, and ask yourself—what does it mean to be a leader in the modern era?

Introduction: The Man Behind the Mask

Alon Mask is not just a name; it is a symbol of the modern era. A name that echoes in boardrooms, tech conferences, and even on social media platforms, where millions follow his every move. Some see him as a visionary, an inventor who is shaping the future. Others see him as a controversial figure, a person who pushes boundaries, sometimes too far. Regardless of how people perceive him, one thing is clear: Alon Mask has become a central figure in today's world, and his story is one of ambition, brilliance, and complexity.

Born into a modest family, Alon was different from an early age. He was fascinated by machines and technology, always curious about how things worked. As a child, he would often take apart gadgets just to see if he could put them back together. This curiosity, combined with a hunger to solve problems, set the foundation for his journey to becoming a tech mogul. But Alon was not just a boy with a dream. He was determined, restless, and fiercely ambitious. From his early school days, it was clear that he would not follow the conventional path in life.

In this book, *Alon Mask: The Mask Man of the Modern Era*, we will take a journey through the life of this enigmatic figure. Alon is more than just an entrepreneur; he is a symbol of the tension between progress and responsibility. He has achieved immense success in industries as diverse as transportation, space exploration, and digital communication. But with his success comes a trail of controversies, mistakes, and public scrutiny. This introduction aims to set the stage for understanding who Alon Mask is, why people are so fascinated by him, and what his story tells us about leadership in today's world.

The Rise of a Tech Visionary

Alon Mask's rise to fame didn't happen overnight. He started his career like many entrepreneurs, with a small idea and a big dream. His first major success came with the creation of PayTech, an online payment system that revolutionised how people transferred money. In an era when online banking was still a novel concept, Alon saw the potential to make financial transactions faster and more accessible to everyone. The company grew rapidly and was eventually bought by a larger tech firm, bringing Alon his first taste of wealth and fame. But for Alon, this was just the beginning.

After PayTech, Alon's ambitions only grew. He wasn't content with just creating one successful company. He wanted to change the world in a bigger way. This led him to his next ventures, including Jitter, a social media platform, and MaskX, an electric car company. With these projects, Alon aimed to solve some of the world's biggest problems—communication, transportation, and energy. Jitter sought to connect people in a more direct and open way, while MaskX promised to reduce carbon emissions and make the world a cleaner place through electric cars.

Each of these ventures brought Alon more fame, more attention, and more followers. People began to see him not just as a businessman, but as a visionary who could tackle the world's biggest challenges. His charisma and public appearances only added to his mystique. He was often seen as a man who could predict the future, someone who was always one step ahead of the curve. But while many admired him, others began to question his methods, his behaviour, and the impact of his businesses on society.

The Enigmatic Personality of Alon Mask

What makes Alon Mask such a compelling figure is not just his success, but his personality. He is a man of contradictions. On the one hand, he is charming, brilliant, and undeniably talented. On the other hand, he can be impulsive, controversial, and unpredictable. This duality is what makes him so fascinating to the public. People are drawn to him because he is both inspiring and flawed, relatable and distant.

In interviews and public speeches, Alon often talks about his grand vision for the future. He speaks passionately about solving problems like climate change, space travel, and renewable energy. His optimism about the future is contagious, and it has inspired countless people to believe that anything is possible. But behind this public persona lies a more complex individual.

Alon is known for his bold statements and controversial opinions, many of which have landed him in hot water. Whether it's an offhand remark on social media or a public feud with a rival company, Alon's words and actions have often been the source of intense public debate. Some see this as a sign of his genius, while others view it as recklessness. Either way, it is clear that Alon's personality is as much a part of his success as his business acumen.

One of the most intriguing aspects of Alon's personality is his relentless drive. He is known for working long hours, often sleeping in his office to stay close to his work. This level of dedication has earned him both admiration and criticism. Some praise him for his commitment to his vision, while others worry about the toll it takes on his mental and physical health. Alon himself has admitted that his work can be overwhelming at times, but he also believes that it is necessary to achieve greatness.

The Public Fascination with Alon Mask

Why are people so fascinated by Alon Mask? Part of the answer lies in the fact that he represents the modern dream. He is a self-made billionaire, a man who came from humble beginnings and rose to the top through sheer will and determination. In a world where technology is constantly changing and evolving, Alon has become a symbol of innovation and progress. People look to him as someone who is shaping the future, someone who is pushing the boundaries of what is possible.

But beyond his business success, Alon's personal life and public image have also contributed to the public's fascination with him. He is not a typical CEO. He doesn't follow the traditional rules of corporate leadership. Instead, he is outspoken, unpredictable, and often controversial. Whether it's his social media antics, his bold business decisions, or his personal life, Alon is always in the spotlight. This unpredictability makes him a constant topic of conversation, both in the media and among the public.

Alon's willingness to take risks, both in his personal and professional life, has only added to his mystique. He is not afraid to challenge conventional wisdom or to go against the grain. This has earned him a loyal following of fans who admire his boldness and ambition. But it has also made him a target for critics who question his judgement and his methods. Regardless of where people stand, it is clear that Alon Mask is a figure who sparks strong emotions and opinions.

The Controversies and Challenges

While Alon's achievements are impressive, they have not come without controversy. Throughout his career, Alon has faced numerous challenges, both personal and professional. His companies have been involved in legal battles, regulatory issues, and public scandals. Some of his business decisions have been criticised for being too risky or poorly thought out. His social media presence has also been a source of controversy, with some of his posts causing uproar and even legal consequences.

One of the biggest challenges Alon has faced is balancing his visionary ideas with the realities of running a business. As an entrepreneur, Alon is constantly pushing the boundaries of what is possible, but this has sometimes led to problems. His ambitious goals have often outpaced the technology needed to achieve them, leading to delays, cost overruns, and even failures. Critics argue that Alon's vision is too idealistic and that he doesn't always consider the practical implications of his ideas.

Despite these challenges, Alon has remained resilient. He has continued to push forward, even in the face of setbacks and criticism. His ability to bounce back from failure and controversy is one of the reasons why people continue to follow his journey. For Alon, every challenge is an opportunity to learn and grow, and this mindset has helped him navigate the ups and downs of his career.

As we embark on this journey through the life and career of Alon Mask, it is important to remember that this story is not just about success and failure. It is about the complexities of being a leader in today's fast-paced, ever-changing world. Alon Mask's story is one of ambition, risk, and perseverance. It is a story that highlights the challenges of innovation, the pressures of public scrutiny, and the rewards of pushing boundaries.

In the chapters that follow, we will explore the key moments in Alon Mask's life—from his early successes to his most controversial decisions. We will look at the companies he built, the challenges he faced, and the lessons he learned along the way. Through the character of Alon Mask, we will examine what it means to be a leader in the modern era and the responsibilities that come with that role.

This is not a story of a perfect man. It is a story of a flawed, ambitious, and complex individual who has left an indelible mark on the world. As you read through this book, I invite you to reflect on the balance between vision and reality, success and failure, and the power of staying true to one's beliefs, no matter the obstacles.

Welcome to the world of Alon Mask—the Mask Man of the Modern Era.

Showdown

Chapter 11: The Price of Power

Chapter 12: The Man Behind the Mask

Conclusion: The Legacy of Alon Mask

Chapter 1: The Spark of Genius

Alon Mask was always a boy with big dreams. Even as a child, he never thought small. While other children were playing with toys and running around outside, Alon was busy taking things apart. He wasn't interested in playing the games that other boys his age enjoyed; instead, he wanted to understand how things worked. The simple toys most children found joy in were just puzzles for Alon—puzzles he wanted to solve. This curiosity was the spark of something much bigger, something that would one day change the world.

Alon was born in a small town. Life in the town was quiet, and most of the people there lived simple lives. But for Alon, the world outside his little town seemed full of endless possibilities. His parents were hardworking but always encouraged Alon to follow his curiosity. His father, an engineer by trade, often spent time explaining how machines worked, while his mother, a schoolteacher, taught Alon the importance of learning and imagination. These early lessons formed the foundation of his passion for technology and innovation.

Alon's first encounter with a computer happened when he was only ten years old. His father brought home an old, clunky machine that seemed like magic to Alon. He was fascinated by how something so big could make so many things happen with just a few clicks. It wasn't long before Alon started experimenting with the computer, figuring out how to write simple codes and make the machine do what he wanted. The more he learned, the more his fascination grew. He would spend hours in front of the screen, determined to master it.

At school, Alon was a bit of an outsider. While his classmates were interested in sports or the latest trends, Alon was always deep

in thought, lost in his own world of ideas. He would often draw sketches of strange machines in his notebooks or write down complex ideas for inventions he dreamed of creating one day. His teachers didn't always understand him. Some thought he was too quiet, while others worried that his obsession with technology was unhealthy. But Alon didn't care. He knew that he was different, and that difference, he believed, would someday make him special.

Despite his quiet nature, Alon had big dreams. Even as a child, he would tell anyone who listened that he wanted to change the world. He wasn't sure how he would do it yet, but deep down, he felt that he was destined for something great. This belief in himself and his ideas would carry him through many challenges in the years to come.

By the time Alon was twelve, he had already taught himself how to program computers. In those days, the internet was still in its infancy, and information wasn't as easy to access as it is today. But Alon was resourceful. He borrowed books from the library, read technical manuals, and spent hours experimenting on the computer his father had given him. Coding became his passion. He loved the idea that he could create something out of nothing, just by typing lines of code.

Alon's first significant project came when he was just fourteen. It was a simple video game, one that didn't look like much compared to the games available at the time. But for Alon, it was a major achievement. He had created something entirely on his own, using nothing but his knowledge and determination. He named the game *Astro*, a space adventure where players had to navigate through obstacles and reach distant planets. The game was basic, but it was a glimpse of what was to come.

Alon didn't just keep his creation to himself. He sent it to a small software company, hoping they might be interested. To his surprise, they were. They offered to buy the game for a modest sum, which was more money than Alon had ever seen. But the money wasn't what excited him—it was the realisation that his ideas could have an impact on the world. If a simple game like *Astro* could attract attention, what else could he create?

By the time Alon was in his late teens, his love for technology had only grown. He had become obsessed with the idea of using technology to solve real-world problems. He would spend hours thinking about the future and how technology could improve it. He was particularly interested in how the world communicated and how technology could make information more accessible to everyone.

It was during these formative years that Alon developed one of his first major ideas—an online platform that could connect people from all over the world. He called it *InterLink*, a social network that allowed users to share information, ideas, and content in real time. The idea seemed simple now, but at the time, it was revolutionary. The internet was still relatively new, and few people understood its potential. Alon believed that *InterLink* could bring people closer together, breaking down barriers and making the world a smaller, more connected place.

However, when Alon presented his idea to a group of investors, they didn't take him seriously. They saw him as a young, inexperienced dreamer with no real plan for how to turn his vision into reality. Alon left the meeting discouraged but not defeated. He knew that he was ahead of his time, and that one day, people would understand the potential of his idea.

Alon's first real taste of controversy came with his next project. By the time he was in his early twenties, Alon had founded a company called *SkyTech*, a technology firm focused on developing innovative software solutions. Alon's goal was simple: to disrupt the way people thought about technology and its role in society. He believed that technology wasn't just a tool for convenience, but a force for real change.

One of his early projects at *SkyTech* was a piece of software called *Pulse*, a program designed to monitor a person's heart rate and health data in real time. The software would then send this information to a central database, where doctors could access it and make real-time decisions about their patients' care. Alon believed that *Pulse* could revolutionise the healthcare industry by making medical information more accessible and immediate.

But not everyone saw the project in the same light. When Alon announced *Pulse* to the public, the reactions were mixed. Some people hailed it as a breakthrough that could save lives, while others questioned the ethics of collecting such sensitive data. Privacy advocates worried that the software could be used to monitor people's health without their consent, while some doctors argued that it placed too much emphasis on technology rather than personal care.

Alon, however, was unfazed by the criticism. He believed that disruption was a necessary part of progress. He argued that technology could improve lives, even if it meant challenging the status quo. But despite his confidence, the controversy surrounding *Pulse* began to grow. News outlets picked up on the debate, and soon, Alon was at the centre of a media storm. Some labelled him a genius, while others called him reckless.

This was the first time that Alon faced real public backlash, but it wouldn't be the last. The controversy around *Pulse* made him realise that not everyone was ready for the kind of change he wanted to bring. But instead of backing down, Alon saw this as a challenge. He had always been drawn to the idea of pushing boundaries, and now he had a reason to push even harder.

As Alon's career progressed, his ideas became bolder, and so did the public's reactions. With every new venture, Alon seemed to walk a fine line between genius and recklessness. His supporters admired his vision and his willingness to take risks, while his critics accused him of being too impulsive and even dangerous.

One of the most infamous examples of this came when Alon announced his plan to develop a network of electric cars that could be powered entirely by renewable energy. The idea was bold, and for some, it seemed too good to be true. Many doubted that Alon could pull it off, especially given the state of the electric car industry at the time. Most companies that had tried to develop electric cars had failed, and many experts believed that it was a lost cause.

But Alon was undeterred. He founded his company, *MaskX*, and began working on his first prototype. The early stages of development were rocky. The technology wasn't as advanced as it needed to be, and the costs of production were skyrocketing. But Alon refused to give up. He poured his own money into the project, working day and night to make sure that *MaskX* would succeed.

When the first *MaskX* car was finally unveiled, it was met with both excitement and scepticism. The car was sleek and futuristic, but many people questioned whether it could compete with traditional petrol-powered vehicles. Critics argued that the infrastructure for electric cars simply didn't exist, and that Alon was chasing an impossible dream.

But Alon saw things differently. He believed that the future of transportation was electric, and that *MaskX* was just the beginning. He envisioned a world where cars could be powered by clean energy, and where pollution from fossil fuels would be a thing of the past. It was a bold vision, and one that required not just technological innovation, but a complete shift in how people thought about transportation.

In the years that followed, Alon's dream of an electric car revolution slowly started to become a reality. As more people became aware of the environmental impact of petrol-powered cars, interest in *MaskX* grew. Alon's boldness, once seen as reckless, began to be recognised as visionary. But even as he achieved success with *MaskX*, the criticisms never fully went away. There were always those who questioned his methods, who wondered if he was pushing too far, too fast.

For Alon, though, the line between genius and recklessness was one he was willing to walk. He believed that in order to make real change, you had to be willing to take risks, to challenge the norm, and to push the boundaries of what was possible. And while not everyone agreed with his approach, there was no denying that Alon Mask had already left an indelible mark on the world.

Chapter 2: The "Funds Secured" Gamble

By the time Alon Mask had established himself as one of the most revolutionary figures in the tech world, his company, *Mask Corp*, had become a symbol of innovation and the future of transportation. *Mask Corp*, famous for producing sleek, fully electric vehicles, had taken the world by storm. Alon's dream of a world powered by renewable energy was slowly becoming a reality. The vision was clear, but the path was anything but smooth.

Behind the scenes, Alon faced intense pressure. The financial markets, the media, and even his supporters were watching his every move. He had always been known for his bold and disruptive ideas, but with that fame came scrutiny. Investors questioned the financial viability of *Mask Corp*, analysts doubted the company's ability to scale, and the constant pressure from being a public company weighed heavily on Alon. It was during this time of stress that Alon made one of the most controversial decisions of his career: a bold announcement that would shake the financial world to its core.

Alon had always dreamed of taking *Mask Corp* to great heights, but being a public company meant that every decision was scrutinised by shareholders, regulators, and analysts. As the CEO of *Mask Corp*, he was under constant pressure to deliver results, meet quarterly earnings expectations, and maintain the trust of investors. The stock market was an unforgiving place. Each time *Mask Corp* failed to meet expectations, its stock price would plummet, sending shockwaves through the financial world.

Alon hated this aspect of running a public company. He felt that the constant focus on short-term profits was in direct conflict with his long-term vision. He wanted *Mask Corp* to focus on innovation

and groundbreaking technology, not on pleasing investors every few months. But the reality of being a public company meant that he had little choice. Every decision was tied to the stock price, and every mistake had immediate consequences.

For Alon, the stress of managing a public company was taking its toll. He was growing frustrated with the limitations placed on him by the financial markets. He saw the future clearly, but it seemed that Wall Street was always standing in his way, questioning his every move. The pressure was immense, and it was during this time of frustration that Alon began to toy with a radical idea: taking *Mask Corp* private.

On a sunny afternoon, Alon Mask sat in his office, contemplating the future of *Mask Corp*. His mind was racing with ideas on how to free the company from the constraints of being public. He knew that if *Mask Corp* was private, he could focus entirely on innovation without having to worry about stock prices or market analysts. The idea of taking the company private was not new, but it had always seemed like a distant possibility—until now.

In a moment of impulsiveness, Alon took to his favourite social media platform, *twitter*, and sent out a tweet that would send shockwaves through the business world:

"Am considering taking Mask Corp private at 420. Funding secured."

The tweet was only a few words long, but its impact was immediate. Within minutes, the financial markets reacted. Investors were stunned. Was Alon serious? Could he really take one of the most high-profile public companies private? And what did he mean by "funding secured"? The message was vague, but it was enough to send *Mask Corp*'s stock price soaring. Investors rushed to buy shares, believing that they were about to cash in on a major deal.

Alon, sitting in his office, watched the chaos unfold. Part of him felt a sense of satisfaction. He had always been a disruptor, someone who challenged the norms and refused to play by the rules. This tweet, in many ways, was a reflection of who he was—a visionary who wasn't afraid to shake things up. But as the minutes passed, Alon began to realise the gravity of what he had just done. The markets were in turmoil, and questions were being raised about whether his statement was true.

News of Alon's tweet quickly spread beyond the financial world. It became the top story on every major news network, with analysts scrambling to understand what this meant for the future of *Mask Corp*. Journalists speculated about who might be providing the funding for such a massive deal. Was it a private equity firm? A sovereign wealth fund? Some even suggested that Alon himself was putting up the money, though this seemed unlikely given the scale of the transaction.

Investors who had bet against *Mask Corp*—known as short-sellers—were hit hard. The stock price shot up, forcing them to buy back shares at much higher prices to cover their losses. These short-sellers were some of Alon's harshest critics, and many had openly doubted the future of *Mask Corp*. Now, they were in panic mode, scrambling to minimise their losses.

But while some investors celebrated, others were deeply concerned. Was Alon serious about this? How could such a major announcement be made over a tweet, with no official statement or explanation? Financial experts questioned the legality of Alon's actions. The Securities and Trading Commission (STC), the regulatory body overseeing the stock market, began to take notice. This wasn't just a bold move—it was a potential violation of securities laws.

As the dust settled, Alon began to feel the weight of his decision. What had started as a moment of boldness now felt like a burden. In his heart, Alon knew that he wanted to free *Mask Corp* from the constraints of being public, but he also knew that the path he had chosen was fraught with challenges. The tweet had sparked chaos in the markets, and now he had to face the consequences.

In private, Alon wrestled with the conflicting sides of his personality. On one hand, he was the visionary, the man who had always believed in pushing the boundaries of what was possible. He had never been afraid to take risks or make bold decisions, and this tweet was just another example of that. But on the other hand, he was also the CEO of a massive company, responsible for thousands of employees and millions of investors. His actions had real-world consequences, and the fallout from this tweet was growing by the day.

Alon had always prided himself on being different from other business leaders. He wasn't afraid to think big or dream of a future that others couldn't see. But now, he was beginning to realise that there were limits to how far he could push. The markets were not as forgiving as he had hoped, and the STC was now looking into his actions. What had started as a bold move was quickly turning into a legal nightmare.

As the days went on, *Mask Corp*'s stock price fluctuated wildly. Some investors still believed in Alon's vision and held onto their shares, hoping that the buyout would go through. Others, however, began to panic. They worried that Alon's tweet was just a stunt, and that there was no real plan to take the company private. The uncertainty caused the stock to swing up and down, creating a sense of chaos in the market.

At the same time, short-sellers, who had lost millions due to the initial surge in the stock price, began to retaliate. They accused

Alon of manipulating the market and misleading investors. Lawsuits were filed, and the media frenzy only intensified. Alon found himself at the centre of a storm, with critics questioning his leadership and integrity.

Through it all, Alon remained defiant. He believed that his vision for *Mask Corp* was the right one, and he refused to let the critics get to him. But as the legal pressure mounted, he knew that he couldn't ignore the situation forever. The STC had launched an investigation into his tweet, and the possibility of fines, sanctions, or even criminal charges loomed large.

Behind the scenes, Alon and his team were scrambling to figure out a way forward. The tweet had been sent in a moment of impulse, but now they had to deal with the consequences. Alon's lawyers advised him to issue a public statement clarifying his intentions, but Alon was reluctant. He didn't want to back down or appear weak. To him, this was more than just a business decision—it was a matter of pride.

In meetings with his board of directors, tensions ran high. Some of the board members were furious with Alon for making such a reckless move. They argued that he had put the entire company at risk with a single tweet, and that his actions had damaged *Mask Corp*'s reputation. Others, however, supported Alon. They believed in his vision and were willing to stand by him, even if it meant facing legal challenges.

Alon himself was torn. He wanted to stay true to his principles, but he also knew that the situation was getting out of control. The media frenzy, the lawsuits, and the investigation were all taking a toll on him. He was used to being the disruptor, the one who pushed boundaries, but now he was starting to see the darker side of that role. The stakes were higher than ever before, and the consequences of failure were becoming more real by the day.

In the end, the fallout from the "funds secured" tweet was severe. The STC launched a formal investigation, and Alon was forced to settle with the regulators. He agreed to pay a hefty fine and step down as chairman of *Mask Corp*, though he remained CEO. The settlement also required him to have his social media posts reviewed by company lawyers before they could be published—a humiliating blow for a man who had always prided himself on his independence and boldness.

The market reaction to the settlement was mixed. Some investors were relieved that the situation had been resolved without further damage to the company, while others remained sceptical of Alon's leadership. The short-sellers, meanwhile, continued to criticise Alon, accusing him of being reckless and irresponsible.

For Alon, the whole experience was a painful lesson. He had always believed in pushing the boundaries, but now he had come face-to-face with the limits of that approach. The "funds secured" tweet had been a gamble—one that had nearly cost him everything. And while he remained committed to his vision for *Mask Corp*, he knew that the road ahead would be more challenging than ever before.

Chapter 3: A Duel in the Caves

Alon Mask was always driven by one thing: solving problems that others believed were impossible. He saw the world not as it was, but as it could be, and he spent his life striving to turn his visionary ideas into reality. Whether it was electric cars, space travel, or harnessing renewable energy, Alon had a knack for thinking outside the box. His ambition was boundless, and he believed that technology could solve nearly any challenge. However, this drive to solve problems, combined with his impulsive nature, sometimes led him into controversies he hadn't anticipated. One such controversy emerged during a real-world crisis that captivated the globe—the Thai cave rescue.

The rescue mission was a heart-wrenching ordeal. A group of young boys and their football coach had ventured into a cave in Thailand, only to become trapped by rising floodwaters. For days, rescue teams from around the world worked tirelessly to free the boys, but the situation grew more desperate with each passing hour. The narrow, flooded passageways made it nearly impossible to reach the children, and experts feared that time was running out.

Alon, following the rescue efforts from afar, felt compelled to act. In typical fashion, he believed that technology held the key to solving this crisis. In a flurry of ideas and prototypes, he began designing a small, high-tech submarine that could navigate the tight, flooded cave tunnels and potentially save the boys. What began as an act of goodwill, however, soon spiraled into one of the most notorious controversies of his career—a public battle that pitted Alon Mask against critics, and ultimately, against his own impulsiveness.

It was one of those moments when the entire world seemed to hold its breath. The Thai cave rescue had captured the attention of

millions, and updates on the progress of the rescue effort filled every news channel and social media platform. The boys, aged between 11 and 16, and their football coach had been trapped deep within the Tham Luang cave system for days. With monsoon rains pouring down, the narrow, winding tunnels were flooded, making any attempt to reach them a perilous and near-impossible task.

The rescue operation was complex and dangerous. Elite cave divers from around the world had been flown in to assist, but even they struggled against the treacherous conditions. The boys were stranded on a small rocky ledge, kilometres from the cave's entrance, with no way to escape on their own. Each day that passed increased the risk of further flooding or a shortage of oxygen. The clock was ticking.

As news of the unfolding crisis spread, Alon Mask's mind raced. He wasn't the type to sit back and watch helplessly. He was a man of action, someone who believed in using technology to overcome seemingly insurmountable challenges. Alon had always viewed himself as a problem solver, someone who could change the world with a single invention or idea. He felt that his resources and expertise could make a difference, and so, he threw himself into the effort to develop a solution.

In his typical fashion, Alon wasted no time. He quickly assembled a team of engineers and technicians from his companies, including *SpaceDream* and *Mask Corp*, and set to work on a bold idea: a mini-submarine that could be used to rescue the trapped boys. The concept was simple—create a small, lightweight vessel that could navigate the narrow, flooded passageways of the cave system and safely transport the boys one by one to the surface.

The design, which Alon dubbed the "Rescue Pod," was inspired by technology from his space exploration company. It was made of lightweight material, fitted with oxygen tanks, and designed to be operated by experienced divers. Alon believed that the pod would provide a safer and faster way to extract the boys from the cave. Once the prototype was ready, Alon announced his plan on social media, eager to help in any way he could.

At first, the response was largely positive. Many praised Alon for stepping up in a time of crisis and offering a potential solution. The media covered his efforts extensively, highlighting his role as a forward-thinking inventor who was always ready to use his resources for the greater good. Alon, never one to shy away from attention, basked in the praise.

But not everyone shared this view.

On the ground in Thailand, the lead rescuer, Vernon "Vern" James, was focused solely on the rescue operation. A seasoned cave diver with years of experience, Vern had been working alongside other experts to develop the safest possible plan to extract the boys. The conditions were unlike anything he had ever seen, and the margin for error was razor-thin. For Vern, the rescue required careful coordination and precise execution—there was no room for outside distractions.

When Alon's mini-submarine arrived on-site, Vern was sceptical. To him, it was clear that the pod, though well-intentioned, wasn't practical for the narrow and twisting cave passages. The boys had to be brought out one by one by expert divers, and the submarine simply wouldn't fit through some of the tightest sections of the cave. Vern felt that Alon's invention, while impressive in theory, wasn't suited for the reality of the situation.

Vern voiced his concerns publicly, stating that Alon's mini-submarine was "just a PR stunt" and would never work in the cave rescue. His blunt criticism caught Alon by surprise. Alon had poured his heart and soul into developing the pod, and he believed it could genuinely help. He hadn't expected such harsh feedback from the lead rescuer, especially after offering his resources and expertise to aid the mission.

Alon was known for his impulsive nature, and Vern's criticism hit him hard. He had always prided himself on being a visionary, someone who could see solutions where others couldn't. To have his efforts dismissed so publicly felt like a personal attack. Alon, never one to back down from a challenge, took to social media to defend himself.

In a moment of anger and frustration, Alon sent out a tweet that would ignite a firestorm:

"Sorry, Vern, but the guy who didn't even use the sub we offered is a pedo guy. Just saying."

The tweet was shocking. In an instant, Alon had gone from a hero offering help in a crisis to someone making a damaging and unfounded accusation against a respected rescuer. The internet erupted in outrage. The media jumped on the story, and within hours, the controversy had overshadowed the rescue efforts. Alon's tweet was seen as not only reckless but deeply harmful, and the public backlash was swift.

Critics accused Alon of being arrogant and out of touch, while supporters of Vern rallied around the rescuer. It wasn't long before Vern himself responded, calling Alon's comment "unbelievable" and expressing his shock that such a serious accusation could be made so casually. Alon, however, doubled down on his statement, refusing to backtrack. What had started as a disagreement over a piece of technology had now escalated into a full-blown public feud.

The controversy took on a life of its own. Alon's impulsive tweet had not only damaged his public image but also led to legal consequences. Vern, furious over the baseless accusation, filed a defamation lawsuit against Alon, seeking justice for what he called a "vile and baseless slander."

The lawsuit became a media spectacle, with headlines around the world covering every twist and turn. Alon's legal team argued that the tweet was made in the heat of the moment and wasn't meant to be taken literally, but the damage had already been done. The public perception of Alon shifted. For the first time in his career, he wasn't seen as the heroic tech genius trying to save the world—he was now viewed by many as someone who couldn't control his emotions and lashed out in harmful ways.

The legal battle dragged on for months, and the stress took its toll on Alon. He had always thrived in the spotlight, but this was different. This was a battle he hadn't anticipated, and the consequences were far more severe than he had imagined. For Alon, the situation became a reminder of the darker side of his impulsive nature.

Behind the scenes, Alon wrestled with the fallout from his actions. He had always prided himself on being bold and fearless, but now he saw the cost of those traits. His impulsiveness, which had often led to breakthroughs and bold decisions in the past, had now led him into one of the biggest controversies of his life. The public feud with Vern wasn't just a legal battle—it was a blow to his reputation.

Alon struggled to reconcile the two sides of himself. On one hand, he was the visionary, the man who had built a career on taking risks and challenging the status quo. He had never been afraid to push boundaries or stand up for what he believed in. But on the other hand, he was also a human being with flaws, and this time, his impulsiveness had led to a situation that he couldn't easily fix.

For Alon, the entire ordeal became a lesson in humility. He began to see that not every battle was worth fighting and that sometimes, his own actions could cause more harm than good. He had always believed in his ability to change the world through technology, but now he saw that words, too, had power—and they could have consequences just as real as any invention.

As the legal battle came to a close, with Alon eventually settling the defamation suit, he found himself reflecting on the entire experience. The rescue mission had been a success—thanks to the brave efforts of the divers on the ground—but his involvement had been overshadowed by his own words. It was a sobering moment for the tech mogul.

Alon continued to work on his many ventures, but the incident left a mark on him. It was a reminder that even geniuses can make mistakes and that even the best intentions can be derailed by impulsive actions. For Alon, the "duel in the caves" had been a public battle that tested not only his reputation but also his character.

And though the world would eventually move on from the controversy, the lesson stayed with him: sometimes, the greatest battles are the ones we fight within ourselves.

Chapter 4: The Pandemic Battle

As the world faced an unprecedented crisis—a mysterious global pandemic that swept across continents and brought life to a standstill—Alon Mask found himself at the centre of a new controversy. Known for his defiant attitude and disruptive ideas, Alon had always pushed against boundaries, whether in the tech world or in society at large. But this time, it wasn't just about innovation or breaking the rules—it was about public health, safety, and the responsibilities that came with being a global figure.

The pandemic, referred to as the "Global Crisis," affected everyone. Countries imposed lockdowns, businesses shut down, and people were asked to stay home to prevent the spread of the virus. But Alon, ever the rebel, saw things differently. To him, the measures taken by governments around the world were overreactions, stifling both individual freedom and economic growth. He believed that people should be free to make their own choices, and he was determined to keep his businesses running despite the risks.

This chapter explores Alon's struggle between rebellion and responsibility, his handling of the Global Crisis, and the consequences of his actions. It delves into the conflict between his desire to keep his companies afloat and the public health concerns that came with the pandemic, as well as the backlash he faced from critics who believed he was prioritising profits over people's lives.

No one saw it coming. The Global Crisis began in a remote corner of the world, with reports of a mysterious illness spreading rapidly through communities. At first, it seemed distant, something that could be contained with swift action. But as the days passed, the illness spread across borders, turning into a full-blown pandemic.

Cities went into lockdown, hospitals were overwhelmed, and governments imposed strict measures to prevent further transmission.

The pandemic affected every aspect of life. Businesses closed their doors, schools shifted to online learning, and public gatherings were banned. People were asked to stay home, wear masks, and avoid contact with others. It was a time of uncertainty and fear, as no one knew how long the crisis would last or how many lives it would claim.

For many, the lockdowns were a necessary step to protect public health, but Alon Mask had a different perspective. As the head of several major companies, including *Mask Corp* and *SpaceDream*, he was deeply concerned about the economic impact of the shutdowns. Factories were closing, supply chains were disrupted, and millions of people were out of work. Alon believed that these measures were doing more harm than good, and he wasn't shy about sharing his views.

From the moment the lockdowns were announced, Alon made it clear that he didn't agree with them. He took to social media, where he had a massive following, and voiced his concerns about the economic damage being caused by the restrictions. He argued that the lockdowns were a threat to freedom and innovation, and that they were disproportionately affecting small businesses and workers who couldn't afford to stay home.

"This virus is being blown out of proportion," he tweeted one evening. *"People need to get back to work. We can't let fear shut down the world."*

The tweet sparked a firestorm. Many praised Alon for speaking out, agreeing that the lockdowns were causing unnecessary harm. Others, however, saw his comments as reckless and irresponsible, especially at a time when the virus was still spreading and public health officials were urging people to stay home. The divide between Alon's supporters and his critics grew wider with each passing day.

But Alon wasn't done. As the pandemic dragged on and the lockdowns continued, he became increasingly vocal in his opposition to the restrictions. He called the virus a "mild flu" and questioned the need for government intervention in people's lives. To him, the solution wasn't shutting everything down—it was finding ways to keep society moving forward, while also taking precautions.

And so, Alon made a decision that would put him at the centre of yet another controversy. He announced that he was reopening his factories, despite government orders to keep non-essential businesses closed. His flagship company, *Mask Corp*, which produced electric vehicles and battery technology, would resume operations immediately. Alon argued that his company was vital to the economy, and that keeping it closed any longer would have disastrous consequences for workers and the industry.

The decision to reopen *Mask Corp* was met with mixed reactions. Some saw it as a bold move—a defiance of government overreach that was crippling the economy. Others, however, were horrified. Public health experts warned that reopening too soon could lead to a surge in infections and put workers' lives at risk. They accused Alon of putting profits ahead of people's health, and the media latched onto the story, turning it into a national debate.

Inside *Mask Corp*, tensions ran high. While some employees were eager to get back to work and earn a paycheck, others were afraid of contracting the virus. Alon tried to reassure his workers by implementing safety protocols—mandatory temperature checks, social distancing measures, and increased sanitation. But for many, the fear of exposure outweighed any assurances that the company was taking the necessary precautions.

Alon, however, was undeterred. He believed that the risks were manageable and that the benefits of keeping the company running far outweighed the potential dangers. In interviews, he spoke passionately about the need to balance safety with economic survival, and he doubled down on his belief that governments were overreacting to the crisis.

"People are smart," he said in a widely broadcasted interview. *"They know how to take care of themselves. We can't let fear control our lives. We have to be willing to take some risks if we want to move forward."*

But as the factories reopened and workers returned to their jobs, the consequences of Alon's gamble became all too real. Within weeks, several employees at *Mask Corp* tested positive for the virus, and the news spread quickly. Critics pounced on the reports, accusing Alon of endangering his workers and flouting public health guidelines. The backlash intensified, with some calling for the factory to be shut down immediately and others demanding that Alon be held accountable for his actions.

As the controversy grew, so did the divide between Alon's vision of freedom and the reality of the pandemic. To Alon, the lockdowns represented an unacceptable infringement on individual liberty and economic progress. He believed that people should have the right to decide for themselves whether they wanted to stay home or go to work, and that innovation should never be constrained by government-imposed limits.

But for many, the stakes were higher than economic freedom. The virus was still spreading, and the death toll continued to rise. Public health officials urged caution, arguing that reopening too soon would only prolong the crisis and result in more lives lost.

To them, Alon's actions were reckless, driven more by his desire to keep his companies afloat than by any real concern for the health and safety of the public.

The tension between rebellion and responsibility was something Alon wrestled with privately. He was a man who had built his career on taking risks and challenging the status quo, but this time, the consequences of his actions were far more serious. It wasn't just about business or technology—it was about human lives.

Alon felt that the media had painted him as a villain, someone who cared more about money than people. But in his heart, he believed that he was doing the right thing. He saw himself as a protector of progress, someone who refused to let fear and bureaucracy stand in the way of innovation. He argued that his decision to reopen the factories wasn't about greed—it was about survival. If the economy collapsed, millions of people would suffer, and he believed that his companies played a crucial role in preventing that from happening.

But even as Alon defended his actions, the criticism continued. Public opinion was sharply divided. Some saw him as a hero standing up against government overreach, while others viewed him as a dangerous figure who was willing to gamble with people's lives. The debate over freedom versus responsibility raged on, with Alon at the centre of it all.

As the weeks passed, the situation grew more complicated. Infection rates in some regions began to rise again, and public health experts pointed to Alon's decision to reopen his factories as an example of what could happen when businesses ignored safety guidelines. Several workers at *Mask Corp* filed complaints, alleging that the company had failed to provide adequate protection and that they had been forced to choose between their health and their jobs.

Alon, for his part, refused to back down. He continued to argue that the pandemic was being blown out of proportion and that the real danger lay in shutting down the economy for too long. He insisted that his companies were following all necessary safety protocols, and he accused the media of sensationalising the situation to make him look bad.

But the backlash wasn't just coming from the media or public health officials. Even within Alon's inner circle, there were those who questioned his decisions. Some of his closest advisers worried that he was taking too big a risk, not just for his companies but for his reputation. They urged him to reconsider his stance, to take a more cautious approach in the face of the ongoing crisis. But Alon, ever the rebel, refused to be swayed.

"I've built my career on taking risks," he told one adviser during a tense meeting. *"This is no different. We can't sit back and do nothing while the world falls apart. We have to keep moving forward, no matter what the cost."*

As the Global Crisis continued, Alon found himself reflecting on the choices he had made. He had always believed in the power of freedom, in the importance of pushing boundaries and challenging conventional thinking. But now, faced with the reality of a pandemic, he began to realise that there was more at stake than just business or innovation.

The world was changing, and Alon Mask was forced to confront a difficult truth: sometimes, rebellion comes with a cost. Sometimes, the fight for freedom must be tempered with responsibility.

And as the pandemic raged on, Alon knew that his greatest challenge was yet to come.

Chapter 5: The Union Uprising

As the world slowly recovered from the mysterious global pandemic, new challenges emerged for Alon Mask and his empire. Alon had weathered storms before—media backlash, government criticism, and even public health crises—but the latest challenge he faced was more personal. It wasn't about technology, innovation, or even the health of his companies. It was about the people who worked for him. Workers in his factories, the backbone of his operations, were beginning to demand change, and it came in the form of a movement that Alon had long been wary of: unionisation.

In the months following the pandemic, whispers of dissatisfaction had begun to grow louder within the walls of *Mask Corp* and *SpaceDream*. Workers, who had been pushed to their limits during the crisis, were calling for better working conditions, fair wages, and more job security. They believed that, despite Alon's vision for the future and his focus on innovation, they were being left behind. And now, they were ready to take a stand.

The rumblings of unrest had been building for some time. For years, Alon's factories had operated at a frenetic pace, pushing the boundaries of what was possible in manufacturing. At *Mask Corp*, the production of electric vehicles had skyrocketed, with Alon determined to meet ever-increasing demand. Over at *SpaceDream*, his space exploration company, workers were constantly under pressure to meet ambitious timelines for rocket launches and space missions.

In the early days of Alon's rise to prominence, his employees had been inspired by his vision. They believed in his mission to change the world, to create sustainable energy solutions and

explore the cosmos. But as the years went on, that inspiration began to wane. Workers felt the strain of long hours, demanding production schedules, and what they saw as a lack of consideration for their well-being.

The pandemic had only heightened these concerns. While many companies had scaled back operations during the crisis, Alon had pushed forward, keeping his factories open and running at full capacity. He had implemented safety protocols, but the pressure to meet production targets hadn't eased. Workers were exhausted, and many felt that they were being treated as expendable resources in Alon's grand vision.

It was in this environment that talk of unionisation began to spread. Workers at *Mask Corp* and *SpaceDream* started to organise, discussing the possibility of forming unions to protect their rights and demand better treatment. They wanted safer working conditions, more reasonable hours, and a say in the decisions that affected their jobs.

For Alon, this was a nightmare scenario. He had always been fiercely opposed to unions, believing that they stifled innovation and created inefficiencies. In his view, unions were relics of the past, outdated institutions that had no place in a company built on cutting-edge technology and forward-thinking ideas. He saw unionisation as a threat to the speed and agility of his operations, and he was determined to stop it.

From the beginning, Alon had made his position on unions clear. He believed that the best way to run a company was to maintain flexibility and control. To him, unions represented bureaucracy, red tape, and a rigid structure that would slow down decision-making and hinder progress.

"Unions are like barnacles on a ship," Alon had once said in an interview. *"They attach themselves and weigh everything down. If*

*you want to innovate, you have to be able to move quickly, and unions
don't allow for that."*

In Alon's mind, unions weren't about protecting workers—they
were about power and control. He believed that union leaders were
more interested in advancing their own agendas than in actually
helping employees. And he feared that if unions gained a foothold
in his companies, they would start making demands that would
compromise his ability to deliver on his promises to customers and
investors.

So, when rumours of unionisation began to circulate within
his factories, Alon moved swiftly to quash the movement. He held
meetings with his top executives, strategising ways to prevent the
formation of unions. He sent out messages to workers, warning
them that unionisation would lead to slower innovation and fewer
opportunities for growth. He even went so far as to suggest that if
workers chose to unionise, it could result in job cuts and factory
closures.

For Alon, the stakes were high. His companies were under
intense pressure to meet production deadlines, and any disruption
to the workflow could have disastrous consequences. He needed his
factories to run smoothly and efficiently, without the added layer of
negotiations and disputes that unions would bring.

But despite his efforts, the workers' demands for better
conditions didn't go away. In fact, the more Alon pushed back
against unionisation, the more determined some of his employees
became.

From the workers' point of view, the situation was clear. They
respected Alon's vision and admired his ambition, but they felt
that their voices weren't being heard. They had been working long
hours under challenging conditions, and many of them felt that

they deserved better. It wasn't just about wages or benefits—it was about feeling valued and respected as employees.

One of the key issues that workers raised was the lack of job security. In Alon's fast-paced companies, employees were often hired on short-term contracts, with little guarantee of long-term employment. This left many workers feeling vulnerable, unsure of whether they would still have a job in a few months' time. They wanted more stability, the ability to plan for their futures, and the assurance that they wouldn't be left out in the cold if business priorities shifted.

Safety was another major concern. While Alon had implemented protocols during the pandemic, workers felt that more needed to be done to protect them on the factory floor. They were worried about exposure to hazardous materials, long hours that led to fatigue and accidents, and the pressure to meet production targets that sometimes resulted in shortcuts being taken.

For these workers, unionisation represented a way to fight for their rights. They believed that forming a union would give them the collective power to negotiate for better conditions and ensure that their voices were heard in decisions that affected their jobs. They didn't see unions as an obstacle to innovation—they saw them as a necessary protection in a rapidly changing industry.

As the push for unionisation gained momentum, workers began to organise more formally. They held secret meetings, distributed flyers, and started petitions calling for union representation. It was a grassroots movement, driven by a desire for fairness and accountability.

The tension between Alon and his workers reached a tipping point when a group of employees at one of his largest factories decided to hold a vote on unionisation. The move sent shockwaves through

Mask Corp and *SpaceDream*, and it quickly became clear that the outcome of the vote would have far-reaching consequences.

For Alon, the vote represented a direct challenge to his authority and his vision for how his companies should be run. He saw it as a battle for the future of innovation—if the workers voted in favour of unionisation, it would change everything. Production schedules would be disrupted, negotiations over wages and conditions would take precedence over technological advancements, and the flexibility that Alon prized so highly would be lost.

In the lead-up to the vote, Alon launched an all-out campaign to convince workers to reject the union. He held town hall meetings, where he spoke passionately about the dangers of unionisation and the impact it would have on the company's ability to innovate. He emphasised the achievements they had made together, reminding workers of the groundbreaking products they had helped create and the role they played in shaping the future.

"We've built something incredible here," Alon told his employees during one of these meetings. *"But if we bring in a union, everything will slow down. We won't be able to move as quickly, we won't be able to take risks, and we'll lose the edge that makes us different from every other company out there."*

Despite Alon's efforts, the workers remained divided. Some were swayed by his arguments, believing that unionisation would indeed slow down the company's progress and jeopardise their jobs. Others, however, were determined to stand up for their rights, convinced that union representation was the only way to ensure fair treatment.

The vote took place on a tense, rainy afternoon. Workers filed into the factory's break room one by one, casting their ballots in a process that felt both momentous and uncertain. When the results were announced later that evening, it was clear that the factory was deeply divided. The vote was close—too close to give a definitive answer. The decision would be subject to further scrutiny, and the debate was far from over.

In the aftermath of the vote, Alon found himself reflecting on the events that had transpired. He was a man who had always prided himself on pushing boundaries and challenging conventional wisdom, but this was a challenge unlike any he had faced before. It wasn't about technology or innovation—it was about people, and the delicate balance between efficiency and fairness.

For the first time, Alon began to consider the possibility that his approach might need to change. He had always believed that unions were the enemy of progress, but perhaps there was a way to reconcile his vision for the future with the demands of his workers. Maybe the answer wasn't to reject unionisation outright, but to find a way to work with his employees, to listen to their concerns, and to build a company where innovation and worker rights could coexist.

The Union Uprising had shaken Alon's empire, but it had also forced him to confront a deeper question: How could he continue to lead his companies into the future without losing sight of the people who made it all possible? As he stood on the precipice of yet another crossroads, Alon knew that the path forward would be anything but simple.

Chapter 6: Betting on the Future

Alon Mask had always been a man ahead of his time. Whether it was electric vehicles, space exploration, or artificial intelligence, his bold vision and relentless drive had disrupted industries and reshaped the future. But as the world became more connected and the digital economy took center stage, there was one frontier that caught Alon's attention with renewed intensity: cryptocurrency.

Cryptocurrency, with its decentralized nature and promises of financial freedom, seemed like the ultimate tool for a visionary like Alon. It was unregulated, uncontrollable, and had the potential to challenge the very foundations of traditional finance. Alon had always been skeptical of centralized authorities, whether they were governments or banks, and cryptocurrency represented a way to bypass those systems entirely. It was a technological revolution that could empower individuals and give them control over their own financial destinies. Or, at least, that was how Alon saw it.

But there was another side to the story, a darker side. Cryptocurrency markets were notoriously volatile, and Alon's interest in the space would soon send shockwaves through the financial world. His tweets, once a source of inspiration and amusement, began to wield an outsized influence over these digital currencies. What started as an experiment would soon become a rollercoaster ride, with some people reaping massive rewards and others left in financial ruin.

Alon's fascination with cryptocurrency began as a side interest. He had long been a proponent of decentralization, seeing it as the future of many industries. His companies had pioneered electric cars, reusable rockets, and artificial intelligence, but he saw

decentralization as the ultimate step towards a freer, more open world.

"Why should anyone have to trust a bank?" Alon mused during one of his late-night brainstorming sessions. *"Why should a government get to decide what people do with their own money?"*

It wasn't long before Alon's curiosity turned into action. He began by diving into the world of blockchain, learning everything he could about the technology that underpinned cryptocurrencies. The more he learned, the more he became convinced that this was the future of finance. Cryptocurrencies like "Bitmask" and "Dogeface" (a playful nod to real-world Bitcoin and Dogecoin) had already captured the public's imagination, and Alon was determined to be part of this revolution.

At first, Alon kept his involvement in cryptocurrency quiet. He made small investments, buying up digital coins and tokens, but his primary focus remained on his companies, *Mask Corp* and *SpaceDream*. However, his restless mind couldn't resist the allure of the cryptocurrency world for long. The decentralized nature of digital currencies aligned perfectly with his belief in individual empowerment and his desire to challenge traditional systems of power.

But as Alon became more deeply involved, he started to see cryptocurrency as more than just an investment or a technology to explore. He saw it as a way to reshape the world, to create a financial system that was free from the control of governments and banks. It was a vision that excited him, but it also carried significant risks—risks that Alon, with his penchant for disruption, wasn't afraid to take.

The first time Alon mentioned cryptocurrency publicly, it seemed like a harmless tweet. Late one night, after hours spent scrolling through online forums and reading about the latest developments in the crypto world, he decided to share his thoughts with his followers. His tweet was simple and lighthearted: *"Bitmask to the moon!"* accompanied by a rocket emoji.

What happened next caught even Alon by surprise.

Within minutes of the tweet, the price of Bitmask, a relatively unknown cryptocurrency at the time, began to skyrocket. Traders, seeing Alon's endorsement, rushed to buy in, believing that if Alon Mask was behind it, the price would soar. And soar it did. By the next morning, Bitmask's value had doubled, and it wasn't long before it became a trending topic on social media.

Alon watched in amusement as the market reacted to his tweet. He had always known that his words carried weight, but this was different. This wasn't just a product launch or a business decision—this was an entire financial market reacting to a single tweet. It was exhilarating, but it also made Alon pause.

"Is this really how the future of finance should work?" he wondered. *"Should markets be so fragile, so easily influenced by a single person's words?"*

Despite his concerns, Alon couldn't deny the thrill of watching the market move in real-time. It was as if he had discovered a new kind of power, one that allowed him to shape the financial landscape with a few keystrokes. But with that power came responsibility, and Alon was about to learn just how dangerous that responsibility could be.

The success of his Bitmask tweet emboldened Alon, and soon he turned his attention to another cryptocurrency—Dogeface. Unlike Bitmask, which was seen as a serious competitor to traditional financial systems, Dogeface had started as a joke. It was a meme coin, created as a playful parody of the crypto world, with no real purpose or value. But Alon saw something in it that others didn't. He saw potential.

In his mind, Dogeface represented the spirit of the internet—chaotic, irreverent, and full of possibility. It was a currency that existed simply because people believed in it, and that, to Alon, was the essence of decentralization. He began tweeting about Dogeface, promoting it as the people's currency, a digital coin that anyone could invest in, regardless of their background or wealth.

"Dogeface is the future," Alon tweeted one morning, followed by a string of dog and spaceship emojis. *"Decentralized, democratic, and unstoppable. To the moon!"*

Once again, the market reacted. Dogeface, which had been trading at fractions of a penny, surged in value overnight. People who had invested early saw their holdings multiply, while new investors flooded in, eager to ride the wave of Alon's endorsement. Social media was flooded with stories of people who had become millionaires practically overnight, thanks to Dogeface.

But as the value of Dogeface climbed, so did the risks. Alon's tweets had created a frenzy, and the market was becoming increasingly unstable. Some people were making fortunes, but others were losing everything. The volatility was extreme, with prices swinging wildly in response to even the smallest hints from Alon.

As the Dogeface craze continued, it wasn't long before Alon's actions drew the attention of regulators and critics. Some accused him of manipulating the market, using his influence to pump up the value of cryptocurrencies for his own gain. Others argued that his tweets were reckless, causing inexperienced investors to pour their life savings into highly speculative assets.

The media, which had once praised Alon for his visionary leadership, now turned on him. Headlines questioned whether he was playing a dangerous game with people's financial futures.

Pundits debated whether Alon was truly a believer in decentralization or if he was simply using his influence to toy with the market for his own amusement.

Alon found himself at the center of a growing storm. On one hand, he believed in the potential of cryptocurrency to create a more open and equitable financial system. On the other hand, he couldn't ignore the fact that his tweets were causing real harm to people. He had seen stories of families who had lost their savings after investing in Dogeface at its peak, only to watch its value crash days later.

The accusations of market manipulation weighed heavily on Alon. He had always prided himself on being a disruptor, but now he was being cast as a villain—a man who played with people's lives for the sake of a few tweets. It was a position he had never wanted to be in, and it forced him to confront a difficult question: Was he really helping to build a decentralized future, or was he just adding to the chaos?

As the market volatility continued, Alon wrestled with his own conscience. He knew that cryptocurrency had the potential to change the world, but he also knew that his influence over the market was creating unintended consequences. People were making life-altering decisions based on his tweets, and that kind of power was unsettling.

Alon's internal struggle came to a head during a heated meeting with his top advisors. Some urged him to stop tweeting about cryptocurrencies altogether, arguing that the risks were too great. Others believed that Alon had a responsibility to continue promoting decentralization, even if it meant facing criticism.

"You're not just an investor, Alon," one of his advisors said. *"You're shaping the future of finance. But you have to be careful.*

People are following your lead, and not everyone understands the risks."

Alon sat in silence, absorbing the weight of their words. He had always thrived on pushing boundaries, on challenging the status quo. But this was different. This wasn't just about technology or innovation—it was about people's livelihoods, their financial security.

For the first time, Alon began to question whether he was truly acting in the best interests of the people he claimed to empower. Was he helping to build a new financial system, or was he simply creating chaos for the sake of disruption?

In the weeks that followed, Alon took a step back from the cryptocurrency world. He stopped tweeting about Dogeface and Bitmask, and instead focused on understanding the broader implications of his actions. He met with experts in finance and regulation, seeking to better understand the risks and challenges of the decentralized future he envisioned.

But even as he tried to rein in his influence, Alon couldn't help but feel a sense of excitement about the potential of cryptocurrency. He knew that the path forward would be fraught with challenges, but he remained convinced that decentralization was the future.

In the end, Alon's foray into the cryptocurrency world was a rollercoaster ride of highs and lows, victories and mistakes. But through it all, he remained true to his core belief: that innovation and progress should never be constrained by outdated systems of control.

Chapter 7: A Space Odyssey

Alon Mask had always been an advocate for a greener planet. His electric vehicle company, *Volt*, was born out of a desire to rid the world of gas-guzzling cars, and his ambitious solar energy initiatives had positioned him as a champion of sustainability. For years, Alon had been hailed as a visionary, someone who would lead humanity into a future where technological progress and environmental responsibility could coexist.

Yet, even as he pioneered green technologies on Earth, Alon's attention had been drawn to the stars. His space exploration company, *MaskX*, was arguably his most audacious venture yet. It was not just about launching satellites or enabling commercial space travel—Alon had set his sights on Mars. He envisioned a future where humanity would become a multi-planetary species, spreading beyond the confines of Earth to ensure the survival of the human race.

But not everyone shared Alon's enthusiasm for this grand space odyssey. Critics pointed out the glaring contradiction between his environmental initiatives and the significant carbon footprint left by his rockets. Each launch, they argued, generated emissions that could harm the very planet Alon claimed to protect. The resources poured into colonizing Mars could be used to combat the pressing environmental crises on Earth.

The tension between his vision of Mars and the environmental concerns it raised soon came to a head, leaving Alon to grapple with the question: Could he pursue his dream of reaching the stars without compromising his commitment to saving Earth?

Alon's obsession with Mars had begun years earlier, during a quiet moment in his sprawling office. As he gazed out at the horizon,

he had been struck by the fragility of Earth—its atmosphere thin, its resources finite. It was a planet that had nurtured humanity for millennia, but it was also a planet in peril. Alon believed that the threats of climate change, overpopulation, and resource depletion would eventually overwhelm Earth unless humanity found a way to expand beyond it.

Mars, with its vast deserts and potential for terraforming, represented hope. Alon believed that colonizing Mars was not just a scientific or technological challenge but a moral imperative. If humanity stayed confined to one planet, it would forever be vulnerable to extinction. But if humans could establish a presence on Mars, they would secure the future of the species, ensuring survival even in the face of catastrophe.

"We need a backup plan," Alon would often say during interviews. *"Mars is that plan."*

His conviction was unwavering, and *MaskX* became the vehicle through which he would pursue this dream. The company had achieved impressive milestones: reusable rockets that dramatically reduced the cost of space travel, payloads delivered to the International Space Station, and even a successful unmanned mission to Mars to test landing capabilities.

But with every rocket launch, the criticism grew louder. Environmentalists and scientists pointed out the massive fuel consumption required to send rockets into space, particularly for interplanetary missions. Each rocket burned through thousands of tons of fuel, releasing harmful pollutants into the atmosphere. The irony was not lost on the public: Alon, the man who had built his empire on green technology, was now being accused of contributing to climate change.

The backlash came to a head after a particularly high-profile rocket launch. *MaskX* had successfully launched its prototype spacecraft, designed for Mars colonization, into orbit. The media celebrated the achievement as a major leap toward interplanetary travel, but environmental groups were less enthusiastic. They called attention to the staggering environmental cost of the mission, accusing Alon of hypocrisy.

"How can you claim to care about the environment when you're pumping tons of carbon into the atmosphere with every launch?" read one scathing editorial.

Alon had faced criticism before, but this time it felt different. The environmental community, which had once embraced him as a hero, was now turning against him. Protesters gathered outside his company headquarters, holding signs that read *"Green on Earth, Red on Mars?"* and *"Save Our Planet Before Colonizing Another!"*

Social media exploded with debates about the ethics of space exploration. Some defended Alon's vision, arguing that the long-term survival of humanity justified the environmental impact of space travel. Others were less forgiving, accusing Alon of prioritizing his personal ambitions over the immediate needs of the planet.

Alon, never one to shy away from controversy, responded with a tweet that only added fuel to the fire: *"Space is the future. If we don't go to Mars, we're just delaying the inevitable."*

The tweet went viral, but the criticism didn't stop. Environmental activists accused Alon of abandoning the fight against climate change in favor of a sci-fi fantasy. They pointed out that while Mars colonization might benefit future generations, it did nothing to address the very real environmental crises facing the planet today.

Behind closed doors, the tension over Alon's dual identity as a green pioneer and space enthusiast was palpable. His closest advisors, many of whom had helped him build his electric vehicle and solar energy empire, were divided on the issue. Some believed that Alon's vision of Mars was necessary and that the environmental costs were a small price to pay for the survival of humanity. Others, however, were concerned that his focus on space was diverting attention and resources from the more immediate problem of saving Earth.

During a particularly heated boardroom meeting, the divide became clear.

"Alon, you've built an entire brand around sustainability and green technology," one advisor argued. *"We can't ignore the environmental impact of what we're doing at MaskX. If we lose the trust of our customers, everything we've built could come crashing down."*

Another advisor chimed in: *"But colonizing Mars is about survival. What's the point of saving Earth if we can't secure a future beyond it? The environmentalists don't see the bigger picture."*

Alon listened intently, his fingers drumming on the table as the debate raged around him. He had always been able to tune out the noise of critics, but this was different. These were his closest allies, people who had stood by him as he fought to revolutionize the auto and energy industries. Now, they were questioning his judgment, and it stung.

"We can do both," Alon said finally, his voice firm. *"We can save Earth and go to Mars. They're not mutually exclusive. If we don't innovate in space, we're leaving humanity vulnerable. And if we don't innovate on Earth, we're dooming ourselves in the short term."*

"I've always believed that technology can solve our problems. It's not about choosing one or the other. It's about pushing forward on all fronts. Yes, rockets create emissions, but we're working on more sustainable fuels. And yes, colonizing Mars is expensive, but it's an investment in our future. We're doing this because we have to. The stakes are too high to back down now."

His words carried weight, and for a moment, it seemed like the room was in agreement. But the tension remained, and Alon knew that the criticism from outside would not go away easily.

As the protests against *MaskX* continued, Alon found himself facing an internal struggle. He had always believed in his ability to balance competing priorities, to find solutions where others saw only problems. But now, for the first time, he wondered if his ambitions were pulling him in too many directions.

On one hand, his work with *Volt* and his solar energy projects had made a tangible difference in the fight against climate change. He had given people hope that technology could solve the world's most pressing environmental challenges. On the other hand, his Mars mission represented a long-term vision that, while noble in its goals, seemed to contradict his message of sustainability.

Alon knew that his critics were not entirely wrong. The environmental impact of space travel was undeniable, and the resources being poured into Mars could be used to accelerate efforts to combat climate change on Earth. But Alon also believed that focusing solely on Earth was a short-sighted approach. Humanity needed to think beyond its immediate needs and consider the bigger picture—survival as a species.

The question that plagued Alon was whether it was possible to do both. Could he continue to push the boundaries of space exploration while staying true to his commitment to environmental sustainability?

In the months that followed, Alon took steps to address the growing concerns about the environmental impact of *MaskX*. He announced a new initiative to develop sustainable rocket fuel, one that would significantly reduce the carbon emissions from future launches. The project, though still in its early stages, was a nod to his critics—a way of showing that he was listening and that he cared about the planet, even as he pursued his dream of reaching Mars.

At the same time, Alon doubled down on his efforts to combat climate change on Earth. He expanded his solar energy projects, investing in new technologies that could accelerate the transition to renewable energy. He also launched a public awareness campaign about the importance of reducing carbon emissions, urging governments and corporations to take more aggressive action.

But even as Alon worked to balance his two worlds, the criticism continued. Environmental activists accused him of greenwashing, claiming that his efforts to develop sustainable rocket fuel were little more than a PR stunt. Others argued that the resources being spent on Mars could never be justified, no matter how sustainable the rockets became.

Alon, for his part, remained resolute. He believed in the power of technology to solve the world's problems, and he refused to let the naysayers deter him from his goals.

"In the end, it's not about Mars versus Earth," he said in a rare interview. *"It's about pushing humanity forward. We can't limit ourselves to one planet, but we also can't ignore the one we have. My job is to make sure we do both."*

The journey ahead was uncertain, and Alon knew that the road to Mars—and to saving Earth—would be fraught with challenges. But he had always thrived on challenges, and this one, he believed, was worth the fight.

For Alon Mask, the future was not a choice between space exploration and environmental responsibility. It was about forging a new path, one where humanity could reach for the stars without losing sight of the ground beneath its feet.

Chapter 8: Tunnel Vision

Alon Mask was never short on big ideas. From electrifying cars and solar power grids to colonizing Mars, his visionary projects were designed to change the way people lived. But there was another idea brewing in his mind, one that seemed more grounded—literally. It wasn't about conquering space or solving Earth's energy crisis, but about something much closer to home: the way we moved.

Every time Alon sat in traffic, he grew more frustrated. Millions of people around the world wasted countless hours in gridlock, breathing in polluted air and burning fuel, all in the name of getting from point A to point B. The inefficiency of it all irritated him to no end.

That's when the idea hit him: Why not take transportation underground?

It was a radical concept, and like all his ideas, it was born out of frustration. But frustration had a way of pushing Alon into action. He envisioned a future where massive underground tunnel systems whisked people and cars from one place to another at incredible speeds, bypassing the snarls of surface traffic entirely. If skyscrapers could make cities expand vertically, why couldn't transportation do the same, but underground?

Thus, *BoreCorp* was born—a company dedicated to digging tunnels. Its goal was simple but bold: revolutionize urban transportation by creating subterranean highways that could ease congestion and bring back the joy of fast, efficient travel.

But as with all of Alon's ventures, this one wouldn't come easy.

Alon's fascination with underground transportation was rooted in his desire to solve real-world problems. He wasn't trying to build something flashy or futuristic for the sake of attention—he was

genuinely annoyed by traffic and wanted to fix it. His pitch to investors and city officials was simple: dig a series of tunnels under cities, connecting key locations with a fast, efficient transportation network.

The tunnels, Alon claimed, could accommodate high-speed pods for people and self-driving cars for private use. Passengers would travel in these vehicles through a vacuum-like environment, reducing air resistance and allowing for incredible speeds. It wasn't quite the hyperloop system he had once proposed, but it was close enough. The idea was that by moving traffic underground, cities could reclaim their streets, and commuting would become an entirely new experience.

"Why should we be stuck in the past with surface-level traffic?" Alon asked during his first presentation of the concept. *"We live in the age of technology. It's time to think differently about how we move."*

The media, as expected, was quick to jump on the story. Headlines praised Alon for his "underground revolution," while others were more skeptical, calling it a "pipe dream." Some commentators couldn't help but roll their eyes at what they saw as another one of Alon's attention-grabbing stunts. After all, they pointed out, he was already juggling multiple ventures—from electric cars and solar energy to Mars colonization and cryptocurrency markets. Could he really pull off yet another audacious project?

The public, for the most part, was intrigued but unsure. Underground tunnels sounded like science fiction, something out of a futuristic movie. How practical could it really be? And more importantly, how would cities—already burdened with old, crumbling infrastructure—handle the kind of digging and disruption this project would bring?

While Alon's supporters were excited by the possibility of zooming beneath city streets at lightning speeds, the critics came out in full force. Journalists and analysts picked apart his plan, questioning its feasibility and branding it a publicity stunt designed to distract from the shortcomings of his other ventures.

One particularly scathing op-ed in a major newspaper declared: *"Alon Mask's underground tunnels are nothing more than a diversion—a way to keep his name in the headlines while his other projects flounder."*

It wasn't just the media who doubted him. City planners and transportation experts voiced concerns about the technical challenges involved in building a tunnel system beneath heavily populated urban areas. They pointed out that existing subway systems, while functional, were already difficult and expensive to maintain. How would Alon's new tunnels—built from scratch—fare any better?

"It's not that we don't appreciate innovation," said one city official during a public forum. *"But this is an enormous undertaking. Digging tunnels under cities is risky, expensive, and disruptive. We need to ensure that public funds are used wisely."*

The question of cost was another sticking point. While Alon claimed that *BoreCorp's* tunneling technology would be cheaper and faster than traditional methods, many remained unconvinced. Some experts argued that the infrastructure costs alone would be astronomical, and the cities most in need of the system—like New York, Los Angeles, and London—were already struggling with massive budget deficits.

Then there were the environmental concerns. Digging tunnels, even with advanced technology, would require a tremendous amount of energy and resources. Critics warned that it could lead to environmental degradation, particularly if it disturbed fragile ecosystems or required significant land excavation. For a man who had built his reputation on green energy, Alon now found himself facing accusations of hypocrisy once again.

Despite the skepticism, Alon was not one to be deterred. He doubled down on his plans, reaching out to city governments in an attempt to secure approval for test projects. His strategy was to start small—building a few tunnels in key cities to prove the concept before scaling up globally.

But dealing with city governments proved to be far more difficult than he had anticipated. City officials, already wary of Alon's bold promises, demanded detailed environmental impact reports, feasibility studies, and cost analyses. They also wanted to know who would foot the bill for any potential overruns.

In Los Angeles, where Alon had hoped to build his first major test tunnel, negotiations quickly became heated. City officials were concerned about the impact on neighborhoods above the tunnel routes. Residents were up in arms, fearing that the construction would disrupt their lives with noise, vibration, and potential subsidence.

One community group even filed a lawsuit against *BoreCorp*, claiming that the tunneling would cause irreversible damage to their homes. Alon, frustrated by the slow pace of negotiations, took to social media to express his displeasure.

"We're trying to build the future," he tweeted, *"but bureaucrats and NIMBYs (Not In My Backyard) are determined to keep us stuck in the past."*

The tweet caused an immediate backlash. Local politicians and community leaders accused Alon of being out of touch with the concerns of ordinary citizens. They pointed out that while he was living in a multimillion-dollar mansion, it was working-class neighborhoods that would bear the brunt of any construction disruptions.

But Alon wasn't one to give up. He shifted his focus to other cities, hoping to find more receptive governments. In Chicago, he had better luck. The mayor, eager to revitalize the city's aging infrastructure, saw potential in Alon's vision. Together, they announced plans for a tunnel system that would connect downtown Chicago to its sprawling suburbs.

The announcement was met with cautious optimism. If Alon could pull it off, it would revolutionize transportation in the city, cutting commute times in half and reducing surface traffic. But the challenges were immense. The city's underground was already a labyrinth of old subway lines, utility tunnels, and sewer systems. Carving out space for Alon's high-speed tunnels would require an engineering feat of epic proportions.

Building tunnels was not as simple as digging a hole. It required precise engineering, advanced machinery, and the ability to navigate around—or sometimes through—existing infrastructure. Alon's team at *BoreCorp* had developed cutting-edge tunnel-boring machines that they claimed could dig faster and more efficiently than anything on the market. These machines were designed to be fully automated, reducing the need for large crews and minimizing human error.

But even with the best technology, the process was slow and fraught with obstacles. In Los Angeles, the rocky terrain and earthquake-prone geology made tunneling particularly risky. Engineers had to design special reinforcement systems to ensure that the tunnels wouldn't collapse in the event of a seismic event.

In Chicago, the challenge was more about space. The city's underground was already crowded with old infrastructure, and Alon's team had to work around it without disrupting essential services. Every inch of tunnel had to be carefully mapped and planned, and even a small miscalculation could cause delays that would cost millions.

Then there was the problem of scaling. Alon's vision wasn't just for a few tunnels here and there—he wanted to create an entire underground network that could connect cities, suburbs, and even countries. But building a single tunnel could take years, and the cost of expanding such a system globally was mind-boggling.

Alon remained undeterred. He saw the challenges not as obstacles but as opportunities to innovate. His engineers were constantly tweaking their designs, testing new materials, and refining their boring machines. Alon believed that once they perfected the technology, the process would become faster, cheaper, and more efficient.

But time was not on his side. The public was growing impatient, and the media was quick to pounce on any delays or setbacks. Headlines like *"Alon's Underground Dreams Falling Apart?"* became more common as the months dragged on without significant progress.

Despite the challenges, Alon refused to back down. He believed in his vision with an almost fanatical intensity. To him, the underground revolution wasn't just about transportation—it was about rethinking the way cities were built. If he could prove that underground tunnels were a viable alternative to surface streets, it would change everything. Cities could become greener, less congested, and more efficient.

"We need to stop thinking about cities in two dimensions," Alon said during an interview. *"The future is multi-dimensional. We can build up, and we can build down. Why limit ourselves?"*

But as his critics grew louder, Alon couldn't help but wonder if they were right. Had he bitten off more than he could chew? Was the underground revolution truly feasible, or was it just another one of his overly ambitious dreams?

The answer, as always, lay in the future. Alon Mask was no stranger to doubt, and he knew that the only way to silence his critics was to prove them wrong. Whether he succeeded in building his underground empire or not, one thing was certain: Alon would never stop pushing the boundaries of what was possible.

As the first tunnel opened in Chicago, transporting passengers at speeds they had never experienced underground, the world watched closely. Would this be the beginning of a transportation revolution, or just another chapter in Alon's long history of daring ideas?

Only time would tell.

Chapter 9: The Neural Network Dilemma

Alon Mask had always been fascinated by the intersection of humanity and technology. He believed that the human brain, in all its complexity, was still fundamentally limited by its biological nature. For years, he had spoken of the potential to merge the mind with machines, creating a symbiosis between human intelligence and artificial intelligence. This idea was no longer the stuff of science fiction. With his new venture, *NeuroLink*, Alon sought to bring that vision to life.

The concept behind *NeuroLink* was deceptively simple: a small implant in the brain, connected to a neural interface, that could communicate with computers, enhance human cognitive abilities, and potentially cure neurological conditions. Alon dreamed of a world where paralysis could be reversed, dementia could be cured, and humans could control technology with just their thoughts. He envisioned a future where the brain could be upgraded like a smartphone, with software updates that would sharpen memory, improve focus, or even boost creativity.

But as with all of Alon's grand visions, this one was met with skepticism, fear, and, increasingly, ethical outrage.

The Promises of the Mind-Machine Merger

In the beginning, the promise of *NeuroLink* was intoxicating. The idea that technology could help unlock the full potential of the human brain captured the public's imagination. Alon framed it as a revolution not just for science but for humanity. He spoke about using the technology to help those with disabilities regain control over their bodies, allowing people who had lost limbs to move prosthetics with their minds. For those suffering from degenerative diseases like Alzheimer's, *NeuroLink* offered the tantalizing hope of restoring lost memories or preventing cognitive decline altogether.

"Imagine a world where your mind is your greatest tool," Alon said during the launch of *NeuroLink*. *"We're not just talking about curing diseases. We're talking about expanding the possibilities of what it means to be human."*

The idea of linking the brain with technology wasn't new, but Alon's ability to make the fantastical seem feasible gave the project an air of inevitability. People wanted to believe that this was the next step in human evolution—a way to transcend the limitations of biology and merge with the machines that were becoming more integrated into daily life.

But the excitement around *NeuroLink* quickly gave way to darker questions. How far should technology go when it comes to blending with the human mind? Was there a moral boundary that shouldn't be crossed, even in the name of progress? And most importantly, who would hold the power in a world where minds could be manipulated by machines?

The ethical concerns around *NeuroLink* began quietly at first, with whispers in academic circles and think tanks. Neuroscientists, ethicists, and philosophers began to raise questions about the implications of the technology. It wasn't long before these concerns grew into a full-blown public debate.

The primary concern was the sheer power that *NeuroLink* would grant its users. If people could control computers, cars, or even other devices with their thoughts, it would undoubtedly change society—but would it do so for the better? Some argued that the technology could be abused, leading to a world where people's thoughts could be hacked, their minds controlled, or their privacy violated in ways that were previously unimaginable.

"We're not just talking about technological enhancement," one ethics professor wrote in a popular op-ed. *"We're talking about the potential for corporations to literally get inside our heads. Who gets to decide what thoughts are private and what can be manipulated? What happens when your mind is no longer your own?"*

The question of control became central to the debate. Alon had always spoken about *NeuroLink* in idealistic terms—helping humanity reach new heights—but many began to see the darker side. If a single company controlled the technology that could interface with the brain, they argued, it could lead to an unprecedented concentration of power. Governments, corporations, and even hackers could have the ability to influence thoughts, memories, and emotions.

Alon, of course, dismissed these concerns. In his mind, *NeuroLink* was about empowerment, not control. He envisioned a future where people could choose how to enhance their brains, much like they chose what apps to download on their phones. But he couldn't ignore the growing public anxiety.

Then came the controversy over animal testing.

From the beginning, *NeuroLink* had conducted its experiments on animals, primarily primates. These tests were necessary, Alon insisted, to ensure the safety and efficacy of the technology before moving on to human trials. But as the project gained more attention, so too did the scrutiny of its methods.

Animal rights groups, already wary of Alon's ambitions, began protesting outside *NeuroLink*'s headquarters. They accused the company of conducting cruel and unnecessary experiments on animals, claiming that many of the test subjects suffered severe side effects, including brain damage and death.

One particular experiment involving a primate named Max ignited a firestorm. Leaked videos showed Max struggling to control his motor functions after receiving a *NeuroLink* implant. The footage, spread across social media, led to outrage. Protests erupted in cities around the world, with signs that read: *"NeuroLink: At What Cost?"* and *"Stop Playing God with Animals!"*

Animal rights organizations called for a halt to all animal testing, demanding transparency from *NeuroLink* and a full investigation into the conditions under which the animals were being kept.

Alon found himself in the eye of the storm. His once hopeful vision of curing diseases and expanding human potential was now tainted by accusations of cruelty and reckless experimentation. In a rare public statement, he addressed the controversy head-on.

"I understand the concerns, and we are committed to ensuring the highest standards of care for the animals involved in our research," Alon said. *"But we cannot make progress without testing. The work we're doing will save plenty of lives in the future. We are not playing God. We are trying to help humanity."*

The protests, however, did not subside. For many, Alon's words rang hollow. The question lingered: Was scientific progress worth the suffering of innocent animals? And if *NeuroLink* could do this to animals, what might it one day do to humans?

The animal testing controversy wasn't just about the treatment of animals—it raised deeper questions about the ethics of scientific progress. As *NeuroLink* moved closer to human trials, people began to ask: What rights do individuals have when it comes to their own brains? Should there be limits on how far technology can go in altering the human mind?

Alon was caught in a difficult position. On the one hand, he genuinely believed that *NeuroLink* could change the world for the better. He had always been driven by a desire to push the boundaries of what was possible, and the potential benefits of

NeuroLink—curing diseases, enhancing cognitive abilities, and even achieving a form of mind-machine symbiosis—were too great to ignore.

But on the other hand, he couldn't ignore the growing unease. The ethical dilemmas surrounding *NeuroLink* weighed heavily on him. As he read the headlines and watched the protests grow larger, he began to wrestle with the moral implications of his work.

Was he truly helping humanity, or was he pushing the boundaries of science too far? Could he justify the suffering of animals—and potentially humans—in the name of progress? Alon had always prided himself on being a visionary, but now he found himself questioning the cost of that vision.

The power of *NeuroLink* lay not just in its ability to interface with the brain, but in its potential to reshape society. If the technology worked as Alon hoped, it could lead to a world where the mind was no longer a closed system. People could share thoughts, control machines with their minds, and even enhance their intelligence. But this power came with risks.

As more people began to consider the ethical implications of *NeuroLink*, some worried that it could create a new kind of inequality. Those who could afford the technology would have access to enhanced cognitive abilities, while those who couldn't might be left behind. It raised the specter of a future where the rich could upgrade their minds, creating a cognitive divide between the haves and the have-nots.

Alon was aware of these concerns, but he believed that *NeuroLink* could be democratized. In his ideal world, the technology would be accessible to everyone, not just the wealthy. But even he knew that the path to that future was fraught with challenges.

Wrestling with the Moral Weight

As the controversy around *NeuroLink* intensified, Alon found himself at a crossroads. He had always believed that technology was the key to solving humanity's greatest problems, but now he was forced to confront the fact that not all progress was without cost.

In private, Alon began to wrestle with the moral weight of his inventions. Late at night, he would sit in his office, staring at the neural interface prototypes scattered across his desk. He had built his career on pushing the boundaries of what was possible, but now he wondered if he had pushed too far.

Was he helping to build a better future, or was he playing with people's lives?

The question haunted him. As protests raged outside his office and debates about the ethics of *NeuroLink* dominated the headlines, Alon knew that he couldn't ignore the concerns. But he also knew that he couldn't stop. The potential of *NeuroLink* was too great to abandon.

"I can't let fear stop progress," he told himself. *"But I can't ignore the consequences either."*

Alon Mask had always been a man of contradictions—a visionary who sometimes ignored the ethical dilemmas in pursuit of his goals. Now, as he stood on the precipice of the most controversial project of his career, he knew that the path forward would not be easy.

The *NeuroLink* dilemma was not just about technology; it was about the very nature of progress. And as Alon grappled with the moral implications of his work, he realized that the future he was building was more uncertain than ever.

Chapter 10: The Social Network Showdown

Alon Mask stared at the holographic screens lighting up the walls of his office, a dozen live feeds of conversations and debates flashing across the platform he'd just acquired. In his hands lay the control to one of the most powerful tools in modern society: global communication. It wasn't just a social media platform anymore. It was the digital town square, the pulse of the modern world. And now it belonged to him.

The platform, *Chirp*, was once a beacon of connectivity, a place where people from every corner of the planet could share ideas, voice opinions, and build communities. But in recent years, it had lost its way. Faced with growing accusations of censorship, biased moderation, and the toxic nature of online discourse, *Chirp* had become a battleground of conflicting ideologies. As user growth stagnated and its stock value plummeted, the platform's leadership had grown desperate. That's when Alon Mask had swooped in with an offer too irresistible to refuse.

For Alon, buying *Chirp* wasn't just another business acquisition. It was a declaration of war on what he believed was a growing problem with global communication—restrictions on free speech. He saw *Chirp* as a platform that had once promised openness but had become a place where voices were silenced and ideas suppressed. Now, in his hands, he envisioned turning it into a sanctuary for unfiltered expression, where people could speak freely without the constraints of what he viewed as politically correct oversight.

But that vision, as bold as it was, would soon plunge the platform—and the world—into chaos.

From the moment the deal was announced, Alon's acquisition of *Chirp* sparked global headlines. The world's richest and most controversial entrepreneur, already entrenched in space exploration, brain-machine interfaces, and electric cars, was now in control of a social network with hundreds of millions of users. The reactions were swift and polarized.

Supporters hailed him as a "free speech warrior," someone who would break the chains of censorship and allow people to express their true thoughts without fear of being banned or shadowed by algorithms. His detractors, however, warned that the platform would become a breeding ground for misinformation, hate speech, and societal division. They feared what unchecked speech in the digital age could do, especially under the control of someone as unpredictable as Alon.

The first day Alon took control of *Chirp*, he fired the executive team, installed his own handpicked leadership, and began implementing sweeping changes. His primary mission: to allow anyone and everyone to speak their mind. This included the immediate reinstatement of previously banned accounts—individuals, groups, and even bots that had been removed for promoting extremism, hate speech, or misinformation.

His reasoning? He believed the platform had gone too far in policing what people could say. In his first public post as the new owner of *Chirp*, Alon declared:

"Censorship in the digital world is still censorship. We must protect the right to speak freely—even if we don't agree with what's being said."

It was a bold statement, one that resonated with many and terrified others.

Within hours of the reinstatements, the platform was flooded with noise. Accounts that had been silent for years sprang back to life, filling timelines with inflammatory rhetoric, conspiracy theories, and vitriolic political debates. *Chirp* was transformed overnight from a relatively regulated space into a digital Wild West.

The algorithms, once tuned to downplay controversial content, were rewritten to be neutral. No more prioritizing "trustworthy" sources, no more suppressing "controversial" topics. Everything was fair game, and the platform's engagement skyrocketed. People were drawn to the drama, the chaos, the uncensored nature of it all. But with that came the darker side—waves of harassment, personal attacks, and targeted disinformation campaigns.

Journalists were quick to seize on the fallout. Headlines read:

"Chirp Descends Into Madness: Alon Mask's Free Speech Experiment Gone Awry"

"Misinformation Reigns as Alon Mask Removes the Filters from Chirp"

"A Platform for All: Or Just a Playground for Extremists?"

The platform, once a place for sharing lighthearted memes and everyday thoughts, was now dominated by battles of ideology. Politicians, activists, and influencers engaged in public shouting matches, their posts amplified by a system that now rewarded sensationalism over subtlety.

Amid the chaos, one question echoed in both the media and the minds of *Chirp* users:

"Does freedom of speech mean freedom from consequences?"

The more *Chirp* grew under Alon's leadership, the more it mirrored the divisions in the world. Nations began to take sides. In some countries, *Chirp* was lauded as a bastion of free expression, a tool for the people to speak out against corrupt governments or oppressive regimes. In others, it was viewed as a destabilizing force, a platform that amplified dangerous rhetoric and fueled societal unrest.

As political movements and fringe groups found a home on *Chirp*, governments grew increasingly uneasy. Some countries threatened to ban the platform outright, accusing Alon of undermining democracy and sowing discord. They pointed to the fact that disinformation campaigns were being waged unchecked, spreading rumors that influenced elections, public health decisions, and even financial markets.

Chirp had become both a tool of liberation and a weapon of chaos.

Behind the scenes, Alon found himself walking a tightrope. He believed passionately in the freedom of speech, but as the consequences of his actions became clearer, he couldn't ignore the impact his platform was having on the world. It wasn't just about allowing people to speak freely—it was about what those words were doing to society.

The platform was polarizing populations, creating echo chambers where people only interacted with others who shared their views. The global conversation was becoming more fractured, and with each passing day, it seemed like the divide between people was growing deeper.

As *Chirp* became more volatile, critics began to accuse Alon of manipulating the platform for his own ends. Some claimed that by removing moderation and allowing chaos to reign, he was intentionally destabilizing global communication. Others accused him of turning *Chirp* into a playground for his personal views, suggesting that the changes he made were less about free speech and more about pushing his own ideological agenda.

The biggest controversy came when it was revealed that Alon had directly intervened in the algorithms, boosting certain types of content while suppressing others. Though he had publicly promised neutrality, leaks from within the company suggested that he had given preferential treatment to accounts and ideas he personally agreed with, while quietly downranking content that went against his vision of the future.

In response to the accusations, Alon was defiant.

"The algorithm is neutral," he tweeted. *"If people don't like what's being said, they don't have to listen. But silencing voices is not the answer. We must let the marketplace of ideas decide."*

But the trust in his leadership was eroding. Many began to see Alon as a tech mogul who, despite his rhetoric of empowering free speech, was wielding his platform as a tool to reshape the world according to his own vision.

For Alon, the *Chirp* acquisition had started as a mission to protect free speech, but it was quickly becoming a burden. As the backlash mounted, he found himself questioning the wisdom of his decisions. He had always believed that more speech was better than less, that people could navigate their way through conflicting ideas and reach the truth. But now he wasn't so sure.

Late at night, in the solitude of his office, Alon scrolled through the platform he now controlled. He saw the hate, the division, the vitriol that had become so common. He saw how people were tearing each other apart with words. And for the first time, he wondered if he had made a terrible mistake.

The world was more connected than ever, but it was also more divided. And Alon Mask, the man who had built rockets to take humans to Mars and dreamed of connecting brains to machines, was now grappling with the reality that his latest venture might be the most dangerous one yet.

Chirp had become a battleground for ideas, but Alon couldn't help but feel that something was being lost in the noise. In his

pursuit of free speech, had he sacrificed the very thing he had set
out to protect? Was it possible that too much freedom, too little
moderation, could be just as harmful as censorship?

The questions haunted him, but the answers remained elusive.

In the end, Alon knew that he held more power than any individual
should over global communication. He had created a platform that
could shape the way people thought, the way they interacted with
each other, and even the way they viewed the world. It was a heavy
responsibility, and as much as he believed in free speech, he
couldn't ignore the fact that words had consequences.

As the platform continued to grow, Alon found himself at a
crossroads once again. Would he continue down the path of
unfettered free speech, allowing *Chirp* to become a place where
anything could be said, no matter the cost? Or would he step in,
reintroduce moderation, and try to find a balance between freedom
and responsibility?

The world watched, waiting for his next move. And for the first
time in his career, Alon Mask wasn't sure what the right answer was.

What he did know was that the battle over *Chirp* was far from
over. And in the ever-evolving digital age, the line between free
speech and its consequences would only become blurrier.

Chapter 11: The Price of Power

Alon Mask stood in the dim glow of his office, the expansive windows offering a panoramic view of the city skyline. It was a sight he often found calming, a reminder of the world he was helping to shape. But tonight, it felt different. The lights twinkling in the distance reminded him of the millions of lives impacted by his decisions. With every success came an equal measure of burden, and lately, that weight was pressing down on him harder than ever before.

Alon had never been one to shy away from responsibility. He had built his empire on the foundation of risk, innovation, and relentless ambition. But the higher he climbed, the more he began to realize just how steep the price of power truly was.

At just 52, Alon was at the helm of industries that spanned the globe—space travel, artificial intelligence, electric vehicles, energy, and more. His companies were household names, synonymous with technological advancement and daring ambition. From his space exploration company, *MaskX*, to his AI project, *NeuroLink*, to his electric car brand, *VoltCar*, Alon had touched almost every major frontier of the future. Each venture carried its own set of challenges, and each had brought him success. But with that success came responsibility, pressure, and relentless scrutiny.

Running multiple multibillion-dollar companies meant that Alon's time was no longer his own. Every decision he made had multiple effects—on markets, employees, and even governments. He was no longer just an entrepreneur; he had become a symbol of progress and innovation. But symbols, as he knew all too well, were easy targets for criticism.

Alon's face was a fixture on news channels and social media feeds. Every time he spoke, markets shifted. Every tweet he sent out could cause stocks to rise or plummet. People either idolized him or vilified him, and the line between the two was razor-thin.

The world wanted Alon Mask to be everything: a visionary, a savior, a genius. But he was still human, despite how much the world tried to make him into something more.

One of the most draining aspects of Alon's life was the constant scrutiny from the public and the media. Every move he made was analyzed and dissected, every word spoken or written interpreted and reinterpreted by pundits and analysts. He couldn't walk into a room without the weight of a thousand eyes on him, each one waiting for a misstep, a sign of weakness.

News headlines had become a daily reminder of how far he had come—and how much he had to lose.

"Alon Mask: Savior of Earth or Master of Manipulation?"

"The King of Industry: How Much Power Is Too Much?"

"Behind the Curtain: The Real Cost of Alon Mask's Ambitions"

The media painted him as a complex figure—half hero, half villain. In some circles, he was celebrated as the man who was pushing humanity forward, breaking boundaries in space travel and green energy. In others, he was criticized for the environmental impact of his rocket launches, the workplace conditions at his factories, and the ethical implications of his AI experiments.

The pressure wasn't just external. Alon felt it in every decision he made, in every project he took on. He knew that his influence extended far beyond his companies. People were betting their futures on his visions—investors, employees, even ordinary people who saw him as a symbol of hope in an increasingly uncertain world.

But that influence came with a heavy price.

Power, Alon had discovered, was a lonely thing. The more successful he became, the more isolated he felt. His closest friends had become distant, some uncomfortable with his growing influence, others resentful of the success they hadn't achieved. Even within his companies, there were few people he could truly confide in. He was surrounded by advisors, engineers, and scientists, but few understood the unique pressure of being the figurehead for so many industries at once.

Alon's family life had also taken a toll. His relationship with his children was strained by his long hours and frequent absences. He had tried to be present when he could, but his responsibilities always seemed to pull him away. His marriages had faltered under the weight of his ambitions, each one ending in bitter separation. He hadn't wanted it to be that way, but the truth was, he had always prioritized his work over his personal life. And now, with so much at stake, it was harder than ever to find a balance.

The world expected him to be available at all times, and his personal relationships had suffered as a result. His partners had grown frustrated with his inability to disconnect, to be present in the moment. Dinners were interrupted by urgent calls, vacations canceled due to emergency meetings, and even family events became secondary to the demands of his companies. Alon knew it wasn't fair to them, but how could he step back when the world was constantly knocking at his door?

And so, he kept going—pushing forward, building the future. But deep down, the isolation was growing, and he wasn't sure how much longer he could bear it.

Alon's relentless drive wasn't just taking a toll on his relationships; it was taking a toll on his health as well. The stress of running multiple companies, being in the public eye, and constantly innovating had worn him down. He worked long hours, often surviving on minimal sleep and a diet that consisted of whatever was available in the office kitchen. His doctors had warned him repeatedly about the dangers of burnout, but Alon couldn't slow down. There was always another project, another problem to solve, another challenge to tackle.

Late at night, when the offices were quiet and the world seemed to stand still for a moment, Alon would feel the strain in his body. His hands would shake from the constant tension, his head pounding from the weight of decisions that affected millions of people. The stress had led to chronic insomnia, and he often found himself lying awake in bed, his mind racing with thoughts of his next move.

But even as his body protested, his mind refused to rest. He was addicted to the work, to the feeling of progress. Slowing down felt like giving up, and Alon was not the kind of person to give up.

Yet, there were moments—brief and fleeting—when he wondered if it was all worth it. Was he sacrificing too much of himself for the future he was trying to build? The thought would pass quickly, drowned out by the demands of his companies and the expectations of the world.

But deep down, the question lingered.

As Alon's influence grew, so did the ethical dilemmas that came with it. He wasn't just building companies anymore; he was shaping the future of entire industries. His AI research at *NeuroLink* had sparked heated debates about the role of technology in human lives, with some accusing him of playing God by attempting to merge human minds with machines. Others praised him as a visionary, someone who was pushing the boundaries of what was possible and opening up new frontiers of human potential.

The moral line, however, was becoming increasingly blurred.

Alon knew that his projects carried enormous ethical weight. Every decision he made could impact society in ways he couldn't fully predict. Was it right to push the boundaries of AI when so much was still unknown about the consequences? Was it responsible to continue launching rockets into space, knowing the environmental impact of each launch? And what about the people who worked for him, often under grueling conditions, to bring his visions to life?

These were the questions that kept him up at night. He wanted to believe that he was doing the right thing, that his work would ultimately benefit humanity. But the truth was, he wasn't always sure. The future was uncertain, and Alon had learned that for every step forward, there was a price to be paid.

Leading multiple global companies meant more than just managing day-to-day operations; it meant being the face of change, innovation, and progress. Alon was a symbol of the future, and with that came immense pressure. Every project, every breakthrough, every failure—it all reflected on him.

When things went wrong, as they inevitably did, the world looked to him for answers. If a rocket exploded during a launch, if a factory had safety violations, if an AI algorithm malfunctioned, it was Alon who took the blame. The media would descend, critics would sharpen their knives, and the stock prices would plummet. He had grown used to the constant scrutiny, but that didn't make it any easier to bear.

Leadership was a lonely place, and the higher he climbed, the more isolated he felt. He had become a lightning rod for both praise and criticism, and the weight of that responsibility was suffocating at times.

Yet, despite it all, Alon couldn't stop. He was driven by something deeper than ambition—an insatiable need to push humanity forward. He had built his empire on the belief that the future could be better, that technology could solve the world's most pressing problems. And even though the cost of that vision was high, he wasn't willing to give it up.

In moments of reflection, Alon would think about the legacy he wanted to leave behind. He didn't just want to be remembered as a billionaire or a tech mogul. He wanted to be remembered as someone who had made a difference, who had helped humanity take its next great leap forward.

But as the years wore on, he began to wonder what that legacy would truly be. Would he be remembered as a visionary who changed the world for the better? Or would history judge him as someone who sacrificed too much in the pursuit of progress?

The answers weren't clear, and Alon knew that the future was unpredictable. But one thing was certain: the price of power was high, and he was paying it every day.

Chapter 12: The Man Behind the Mask

Alon Mask stood alone in the shadows of his expansive mansion, staring out at the vast night sky. The stars twinkled above, distant and indifferent, much like his own life felt at that moment. The house was eerily quiet, a stark contrast to the chaos of his workday. For once, there were no ringing phones, no meetings, no press conferences, no demands for his attention. It was just him—Alon, stripped of his public persona, the weight of his empire temporarily set aside.

The silence, though peaceful, felt alien. Alon had grown so accustomed to the constant noise of his life—the hum of innovation, the chatter of business deals, the roar of public scrutiny—that this stillness unnerved him. It forced him to confront something he had long pushed aside: himself.

Alon had always been a man of vision, someone who saw the world not for what it was, but for what it could be. As a child, he had been fascinated by science fiction, by tales of space exploration, artificial intelligence, and the limitless potential of human ingenuity. Those early passions had propelled him to where he was today—the CEO of multiple companies, the face of technological progress, and, in many eyes, a modern-day visionary.

But somewhere along the way, the lines between vision and obsession had blurred. His relentless pursuit of innovation had consumed his life, leaving little room for anything—or anyone—else. The relationships he had once cherished had withered in the shadow of his ambition. His marriages had ended in bitterness and resentment, and his friendships had faded into distant memories. Even his children, whom he loved dearly, felt more like strangers than family.

Alon's personal life had become a casualty of his success, and for the first time, standing alone in the quiet of his home, he wondered if the trade-off had been worth it.

Alon's mind wandered to his children. He hadn't seen them in weeks, despite promising himself he'd make time. They were growing up, shaping their own lives, and he was missing it all. He remembered the excitement of holding his firstborn, the overwhelming love he felt. But that love had been eclipsed by the pressures of his work, by the never-ending demands of being Alon Mask.

His children knew him as a figure on the screen or in the news rather than a father who was present. He had missed school plays, birthdays, even simple dinners because of board meetings or emergency calls. They'd learned to stop expecting him to show up, and that realization haunted him. It was a quiet betrayal, one that wasn't shouted or fought over but accepted with a weary resignation. They didn't resent him outright, but their distance was palpable.

Alon had tried to bridge the gap, to show them that he cared, but his efforts always felt too late, too little. He had become a stranger to his own family, a figure defined by the successes of the public world rather than the personal one.

Then there were his marriages—relationships that had once been filled with passion and love but had crumbled under the pressure of his ambition. His partners had been drawn to his drive, his vision, but over time, that same ambition became the wedge that pushed them away. They grew tired of waiting for him to come home, tired of competing with his companies for his attention. One by one, they left, and Alon was left alone, wondering why he couldn't make it work.

He had always told himself that his work was for the greater good, that the sacrifices he made were necessary for the progress of humanity. But now, as he stood alone in his vast, empty house, he began to question that belief. Had he sacrificed too much? Had he lost sight of what truly mattered?

In the quiet moments, when the meetings were over and the cameras were off, doubt began to creep into Alon's mind. For years, he had pushed forward with a singular focus, convinced that his work was changing the world for the better. But now, as the weight of his empire pressed down on him, he couldn't shake the feeling that something was off. Was he truly making the world a better place, or had his ambition blinded him to the consequences of his actions?

He thought about *MaskX* and the environmental impact of his space projects. The dream of colonizing Mars had once seemed like the ultimate solution to humanity's problems—a way to secure the future of the species. But as the years went by, the criticisms grew louder. Environmentalists decried the emissions from his rocket launches, accusing him of prioritizing space over the planet they already inhabited. Alon had always brushed off those concerns, insisting that the long-term benefits outweighed the short-term costs. But now, in the stillness of his thoughts, he wondered if he had been too dismissive.

The same doubts plagued his work with *NeuroLink*. The project was supposed to revolutionize medicine, to help people with disabilities regain control of their lives. But the ethical questions surrounding the technology—about the merging of man and machine—were impossible to ignore. The protests, the accusations of playing God, the fears of a dystopian future where human consciousness could be manipulated by technology—it was all starting to weigh on him.

Alon had always seen himself as a force for good, as someone who was pushing humanity forward. But what if he was wrong? What if, in his quest for progress, he was inadvertently causing harm?

Alon walked through his home, his footsteps echoing in the empty halls. He passed by family photos, framed reminders of a time when his life was simpler, when his ambitions hadn't yet consumed everything. He paused in front of a picture of him and his first wife, taken on the day they launched *VoltCar*. They had been so full of hope, so convinced that they were changing the world for the better. But that hope had faded, replaced by the harsh realities of the business world.

Alon had always been able to justify his sacrifices, telling himself that the ends justified the means. But as he stared at the photo, he couldn't help but wonder if he had been lying to himself all along. Was it really worth it? Had he truly made the world a better place, or had he simply built an empire at the cost of his own happiness?

He thought about his critics, the people who accused him of being more interested in profit than progress. He had always dismissed them, confident in the righteousness of his vision. But now, in the quiet of his own thoughts, their words began to sink in. Was he really any different from the corporate giants he had once railed against? Had his ambition turned him into the very thing he had once despised?

Alon shook his head, trying to push the thoughts away. He wasn't one to dwell on the past, to wallow in self-pity. But the doubts lingered, gnawing at the edges of his mind.

Beneath all of Alon's bravado, there was a deep-seated fear that he rarely allowed himself to acknowledge: the fear of failure. For all his successes, for all his accomplishments, Alon was terrified that it could all come crashing down. He had built an empire, but empires could fall.

The weight of expectation was crushing. The world looked to him as a visionary, as someone who could solve humanity's greatest challenges. But what if he couldn't live up to those expectations? What if, despite all his efforts, he failed?

Alon's fear of failure wasn't just about losing money or seeing his companies falter. It was about something deeper—the fear that his life's work might ultimately amount to nothing. That all the sacrifices, all the sleepless nights, all the strained relationships might have been for naught.

He had always prided himself on being able to push through adversity, to keep moving forward no matter the obstacles. But now, as he stood alone in his home, he couldn't help but wonder if he was reaching his breaking point.

As dawn approached, Alon found himself sitting on the edge of his bed, staring out at the first rays of sunlight breaking over the horizon. For all his technological advancements, for all the ways he had tried to push humanity into the future, there was something about the simplicity of a sunrise that technology could never replicate. It was a reminder that, despite all his ambitions, he was still just a man—a man with doubts, fears, and vulnerabilities.

In that moment, Alon allowed himself to feel something he hadn't felt in a long time: humility. For years, he had been seen as larger than life, as someone who could change the world with a single idea. But in reality, he was no different from anyone else. He had made mistakes, he had hurt people, and he had lost sight of what truly mattered.

As the sun rose higher, Alon made a silent promise to himself. He couldn't undo the past, couldn't change the choices he had made or the relationships he had damaged. But he could try to be better. He could try to find a balance between his ambition and his personal life, between progress and humanity.

It wouldn't be easy. The world would continue to expect great things from him, and he would continue to push the boundaries of what was possible. But perhaps, just perhaps, he could find a way to do so without losing himself in the process.

For the first time in a long time, Alon felt something stir inside him—a sense of hope. Not for his companies, not for his inventions, but for himself. The man behind the mask.

The Legacy of Alon Mask

Alon Mask's journey had been nothing short of extraordinary. From a young boy with a dream of reaching the stars to a man who reshaped industries and redefined the boundaries of human potential, his life story was a testament to the power of relentless ambition and unshakable vision. He had not only envisioned the future but actively set out to build it—whether through electric cars, space travel, brain-machine interfaces, or free speech battles in the digital age.

As Alon stood at the pinnacle of his empire, his legacy stretched far beyond the confines of his companies. He had altered the course of energy, transportation, communication, and artificial intelligence. He had made daring promises to the world, and though some of those promises remained unfulfilled, his ability to move the needle of human progress could not be denied.

But as the years passed, and the dust settled around his many projects, a question remained: What, exactly, was Alon Mask's legacy?

A Visionary and a Disrupter

Alon Mask's influence was undeniable. In the early days, he was seen as a visionary—a man who dared to challenge the status quo and push the world toward cleaner energy, sustainable transportation, and exploration beyond Earth. His electric vehicles revolutionized the auto industry, forcing legacy automakers to rethink their approach to clean energy. Through *MaskX*, he had brought the dream of space exploration within reach, democratizing the stars for those who had once believed it was impossible.

Alon's innovations in tunneling, AI, and neurotechnology pushed the boundaries of what technology could achieve. He was the kind of leader who thrived on disruption, who believed that shaking up entrenched industries was the only way to progress. And in doing so, he had irrevocably changed the world.

But with disruption came controversy. Alon's methods—his brashness, his unwillingness to compromise, his tendency to overpromise—often left him at odds with governments, critics, and even his own supporters. He was a man who thrived on the edge of chaos, who sought to redefine the rules rather than abide by them.

To some, this made him a hero—a bold leader who wasn't afraid to ruffle feathers in the pursuit of a better future. To others, it made him a reckless disrupter, someone who prioritized ambition over stability, innovation over ethics. His clashes with regulatory bodies, his public spats with critics, and his disregard for traditional norms often led to accusations of hubris.

A Flawed Genius

Yet, for all his accomplishments, Alon was also deeply flawed. The personal toll of his relentless drive was evident in the broken relationships, the estranged children, and the empty spaces in his life that success couldn't fill. His private battles—ones the public rarely saw—were marked by loneliness, doubt, and the haunting question of whether the sacrifices he made were worth it.

Alon's journey was marked by moments of triumph and failure, of brilliant innovation and costly mistakes. His social network takeover, for example, had been a divisive move. While he had championed free speech, his actions led to chaos, polarization, and the erosion of trust on the platform. His brain-machine interface project raised ethical concerns, forcing the world to confront the limits of technological progress and the moral questions that accompanied it.

But Alon never shied away from his flaws. He embraced them as part of who he was, part of the messy process of invention and progress. In his view, perfection was an illusion; it was the willingness to take risks, to fail, and to keep pushing forward that defined success. His critics might have seen arrogance, but Alon saw resilience.

In the end, it was this very imperfection that made him so human. Alon Mask wasn't a paragon of virtue, nor was he a villain. He was something more complex—a man driven by forces that sometimes even he couldn't control, a genius wrestling with the consequences of his own ambition.

A Reflection of the Modern Era

Alon Mask's story was not just the story of a man. It was the story of a moment in history, of a world in flux, grappling with the possibilities and dangers of unprecedented technological advancement. He was, in many ways, a reflection of the modern era—a time when innovation and controversy often went hand in hand, when the race to push the boundaries of what was possible sometimes outpaced the careful consideration of its consequences.

His rise to prominence coincided with an era of rapid change, where technology reshaped industries, societies, and even the way people thought about the future. In Alon, the world saw both the promise and the peril of this change. He was the embodiment of the tech titan—a man who held immense power and responsibility, who could inspire awe and fear in equal measure.

Alon's legacy was intertwined with the ethical dilemmas of his time. Could humanity merge with machines without losing its soul? Could space exploration justify the environmental cost? Could social networks truly be bastions of free speech without spiraling into chaos? These were the questions Alon had left behind for the world to grapple with, questions that didn't have easy answers.

In the end, Alon Mask wasn't just a figurehead for innovation—he was a symbol of the challenges that came with it. His life, his work, and his impact were all reflections of the complexities of the modern world.

Hero, Flawed Genius, or Something In Between?

As the world looked back on Alon's life, it was impossible to neatly categorize him. Was he a hero, someone who had changed the world for the better? Or was he a flawed genius, whose ambition sometimes led him astray? Perhaps he was something in between—a man who had both lifted humanity up and made mistakes along the way.

Alon Mask's legacy would be debated for years to come. His inventions and ideas would continue to shape the future, but so too would the controversies and ethical dilemmas he left behind. In many ways, he was a mirror held up to society, forcing people to confront their own relationship with progress and the cost of ambition.

His story left a lingering question: What does it mean to be a visionary in a world that is constantly changing? Is it enough to have big ideas, or must those ideas be tempered with responsibility? Can one person truly change the world, or is the price of such change too high?

As the book of Alon Mask's life came to a close, these questions remained unanswered. But perhaps that was the point. Alon's legacy wasn't about definitive answers—it was about pushing humanity to think bigger, to question more, and to wrestle with the complexities of the modern age.

In the end, Alon Mask was not a hero, nor was he a villain. He was a man—brilliant, flawed, and undeniably human. And in that humanity, he left a legacy that would continue to shape the world long after he was gone.

Dear Reader,

As I write these final words, I find myself reflecting not only on the story of Alon Mask but also on the broader themes that his journey brings to light. Alon Mask is a fictionalized character, yet his path is one that resonates deeply with the world we live in—a world defined by rapid change, innovation, and the tension between progress and responsibility.

Through this book, I sought to explore the complexities of ambition, power, and human nature. Alon's story is not a simple one; it is filled with triumphs and failures, brilliance and flaws. He is, in many ways, a symbol of our time—someone who challenges the status quo, disrupts industries, and pushes humanity forward, while also forcing us to confront the ethical dilemmas and unintended consequences that come with such innovation.

As we consider Alon's legacy, we are reminded that no individual is one-dimensional. Just like the real-world figures who inspire and shape our society, Alon is a blend of visionary ambition and human imperfection. He is someone who dreams big and works tirelessly to turn those dreams into reality, yet he also struggles with the personal and moral costs of his actions. This duality, I believe, is what makes him both compelling and relatable.

The questions raised in this story are not meant to provide easy answers. Instead, they are intended to provoke thought and encourage discussion. In a world where technology is advancing at an unprecedented pace, we must ask ourselves: What is the true cost of progress? How do we balance innovation with responsibility? And most importantly, how do we ensure that the future we are building serves not just the few, but all of humanity?

As you close this book, I hope you carry these questions with you. The legacy of Alon Mask, like that of any influential figure, will be debated for years to come. But in the end, what matters most is how we, as individuals and as a society, choose to navigate the challenges and opportunities that lie ahead.

Thank you for joining me on this journey. I hope Alon's story has inspired you to think critically, dream boldly, and always strive to make the world a better place—whether through your own actions or by supporting those who dare to push the boundaries of what is possible.

With gratitude and best wishes,
Anshumala Singh
Author of The Legacy of Alon Mask

Don't miss out!

Visit the website below and you can sign up to receive emails whenever Anshumala Singh publishes a new book. There's no charge and no obligation.

https://books2read.com/r/B-A-IYPWB-SLPAF

BOOKS 2 READ

Connecting independent readers to independent writers.

Did you love *Alon mask - Hero, Flawed Genius, or Something In Between?*? Then you should read *Sacred Ambition*[1] by Anshumala Singh!

Every person has a dream, a desire to achieve something great in life. But along the way, we often get caught up in the hustle of the world—seeking wealth, power, and fame. In this race, we sometimes lose sight of the true purpose behind our ambitions. This is where the idea of sacred ambition comes in.

Sacred Ambition is a story about Keshav, a man who, like many of us, starts his journey with big dreams. But as he rises in his career, he faces a question that haunts many ambitious people: Is this all there is? The story is not just about achieving success but about understanding what makes success meaningful.

1. https://books2read.com/u/4X5Xr5

2. https://books2read.com/u/4X5Xr5

I wrote this book with the hope that it will help readers reflect on their own dreams and ambitions. I believe that when we align our ambitions with a higher purpose, our journey becomes not just successful but also fulfilling.

This book is for anyone who has ever dreamed big, faced challenges, and wondered if there is more to life than just chasing achievements. May it inspire you to pursue your own sacred ambition.

Milton Keynes UK
Ingram Content Group UK Ltd.
UKHW030619061024
449204UK00001B/34